Grave Secrets

Short Tales of Mystery and Mayhem

by

Rex Munsee and Jeffrey Vavra

Cover concept by Jeffrey Vavra

Interior art by Steve Swenston

Print Version

Revised April, 2021

Table of Contents

Introduction

First off, my partner-in-crime, Jeffrey Vavra, and I thank you from the bottom of our miserly hearts for spending your time with us. We realize that your time is both valuable and fugacious commodities that you dole out sparingly.

Secondly, sit back and enjoy our riveting and sharp jabbing stories. We've cut out the fat and are presenting some lean tales that will remind you of the best of the pulps with the sensibilities of our modern times. We hope these tales grab you by the throat and force you to furtively glance at the door. If that occurs, we'll feel that our time has been well spent.

Finally, if you truly enjoy these "grave" tales, tell your friends and spread the news. Jeffrey and I have other stories scratching the lids of their coffins, desperately trying to be released.

Rex

Dedication

There can only be one, to my wife, Cindi, with all my love. Thanks for putting up with me for all these years together.

Rex

To Infinity.

Steve

To my children, Grace and Christopher. You continue to amaze and delight me in all that you say and do. I'm proud of you both. Don't be late for Mystery Meat Monday.

Jeffrey

There was a loud meaty THWACK of the wood hitting the leather palm of his glove.

The Seventh Commandment

By Jeffrey Vavra

CRACK! A sound not unlike the snapping of a dry branch.

"Aaaaaaaagh, God, what the hell!?" The scream was loud and magnified in the confined space of the concrete block walls of the MEN'S restroom in the park. The outcry spooked a bird from its nest on a rafter under the restroom's ventilated sheet-metal roof.

"Now we're getting somewhere." The clean-shaven, handsome man dressed in black slacks and a crisp black shirt, squatted down, his chin now resting on the ax handle. "That one definitely broke the bone."

"Uh, uh what the…why?" Through eyes muddied with tears, the terrified man looked down at his lower left leg. His shin had a gash when it had exploded open where the ax handle hit the bone, fracturing it. What movement he could make was excruciating. He imagined he could hear the sound of the jagged ends of the bones as they scraped against one another.

"Bob—or do you prefer Robert? Kay calls you Robert. So I suppose you prefer Robert."

"I…d-do…I-I don't care," he panted. He strained against the handcuffs holding his arms above his head.

The man with the ax handle had waited by the trail for the jogger as he came through an isolated portion of the state park on his regular late-afternoon run. Recognizing his target, he stepped into the path of the jogger. He held a pistol in his black glove-covered hand. The jogger's pleas to be let go as he had no money were ignored and he had been marched off the path a short distance to a park restroom. Once inside the MEN'S room, the man with the gun ordered the jogger to take off his socks and shoes and sit down on the cold, damp concrete floor. He then pulled a pair of police-issue handcuffs from his right back pocket and cuffed the man's hands above his head around a pipe that carried water to the sheet-metal trough mounted on the wall. The gun he tucked into his front waistband.

The jogger regained some of his composure. "In God's name, why are you doing this?"

"In God's name?" The man jumped to his feet in surprise. "Do you know the Seventh Commandment?"

After a moment's hesitation. "Thou shalt not kill?" his prisoner offered in a defeated voice.

"That's number six," was the reply.

The man, dressed all in black, stared at the man on the floor then moved the ax handle from his left hand to his right hand, and pulled from his other back pocket a black silk thong and dangled it back and forth in the face of his prisoner, as a company party hypnotist would a gold watch or a crystal ball on a chain. The jogger shook his head from side to side, as the man moved it closer and closer until it was against his face.

He leaned over and stuffed it in the jogger's mouth despite the jogger's protestations, then stood up.

"Kay didn't start wearing those until she started jogging with you," he said.

He ran his leather-clad hand down the ax shaft as if caressing a woman's arm.

Without warning, he swung the handle down against the jogger's right kneecap, splintering the soft bone.

The silk thong muffled the scream.

The jogger grimaced in pain; the cords of his neck taut against the skin.

The man in black stepped around to the side so he was facing the jogger's left leg. He lowered the ax handle and bent forward so that he could place the end of the shaft against the big toe, then adjusted his stance several times swinging the ax handle back and forth, lining it up with the big toe like a golfer getting set to tee off.

The man on the floor panicked. Gasping and crying, he tried to move his rapidly swelling legs out of the way.

The black-clad man brought his right foot up and placed his black-leather Rockport down with mock sensitivity on the area right above the ankle, firmly holding it in place. The pressure on the leg caused the fractured bone tips to rub against one another, inflicting more pain. He hopped a bit to get his balance and adjusted his stance to line the wood handle up with the big toe.

The jogger's brain sent out a signal to his right leg to use it to push the madman from him, but the signal fell on deaf nerves.

"Ever watch that television mini-series ROOTS by Alex Haley, Robert? Maybe you saw it in a high school class."

The jogger's eyes opened wide. They were surprisingly clear with all that he had endured.

"There was this slave, Kunta Kinte, who ran away. But they caught him and brought him back. The owner of the plantation could have hanged or shot him, but he did something different. You know what he did?"

The man reached over and grabbed the jogger's chin in his hand. "Do you?" he asked.

The jogger's breath came faster and more strained. He

continued to wheeze through his blocked mouth.

"He took ol' Kunta's foot and put it on a tree stump. I can't remember if it was the left or right. It was so long ago," he said, his voice getting softer as he tried to remember. "It doesn't matter; let's say for the sake of argument it was the left. Like the one I'm standing on. Kunta's owner took an ax and chopped the front of the foot off behind the toes."

He brought the ax handle down in a furious arc into his palm. There was a loud meaty THWACK of the wood hitting the leather palm of his glove.

The jogger's body spasmed at the sound and he screamed as best he could through the gag.

Wheezing, the jogger tried to fill his lungs with air, his chest heaved in exertion, his airway still obstructed with the thong. Mucus ran from his nose, mixed with the tears falling from his eyes, and rolled down off his chin.

While he waited for the jogger's breathing to calm, the man in black rhythmically tapped the ax handle in his palm to the cadence of the water drops that fell from the spigot in the sink to hit the bottom of the metal basin. Ping . . . ping . . . ping.

"He did that so Kunta could never run away again. Alive and crippled, the other slaves would see Kunta every day as an example that something terrible would happen to them if they tried to escape."

The man looked the jogger square in the eyes. "And that's what I'm doing, creating an example for my wife. I don't have an ax but I have an ax handle," he said. He brought the handle up quick and ferociously brought it back down like a golfer using his heaviest wood in a longest drive contest.

WHACK!!

The sharpness of the wood's edge bit in below the knuckle of the largest toe and cleaved it clean off, sending it flying across the room to land in a puddle of water that gathered beneath the metal sink.

With his foot still on the jogger's ankle, the man in black adjusted his stance and took one more swing.

"Did you enjoy jogging with my wife or just what you did afterward?"

"NO!" His prisoner screamed, again and again, strangely intelligible through the gag.

SMACK! A wet, slapping sound ricocheted off the metal roofing.

The man in black took a moment to brush back his dark hair from his eyes so he could see as he looked down. Adjusting his stance one more time brought renewed whimpering from the jogger as he brought the wood handle up.

He hit three toes this time. One was almost severed and hung by only a thread of skin, the other two are pulped.

More muffled screams. Then sobbing.

The man dropped the ax handle on the heaving man's chest.

In exhaustion the jogger's head slumped with a metallic clang against the side of the metal urinal.

The handcuffs are unlocked and pocketed and the jogger's arms fell like dead weight.

The man in black walked to the entrance door and from behind it retrieved a metal can labeled gasoline.

The man on the floor watched with a confused look on his face.

"I have to get going. My wife will be getting home soon and wondering why she hasn't heard from you today and she will need comfort in what will be a difficult time for her when she finds out why." From his shirt pocket, he pulled a matchbook. He lit one and used it to light the others in the matchbook, then dropped it. He watched as it seemed to take forever to reach the floor. The fiery tip leading the way like a bullet-riddled WWII Stuka, belching smoke and fire as it hurtled dead weight toward a quick stop with the floor.

Watching the matchbook drop toward the liquid where it pooled around his legs, the man on the floor screamed and threw up his arms in defense while at the same time he tried to roll off to the side, but with his damaged leg and foot, he couldn't get the leverage needed to roll.

The flaming matchbook splashed down into the puddle next to the legs of the panic-stricken man.

And the flame was snuffed.

Removing his gloves the man in black wiped his hands on his slacks, then smoothed his hair back in place, adjusted the white tab of his clergy collar, and walked toward the door.

"Oh, as far as the Seventh Commandment, you've probably figured that out by now, right?"

"I was told that your firm is not averse to writing policies for… unusual clients…"

Life Insurance

By Rex Munsee

The sun had slipped below the horizon, causing the buildings of Chicago to cast shadows upon the storefront on Lou Cypher's Insurance Agency, nestled along a side street, parallel to 146th Street. As the biting wind blew across ice-covered Lake Michigan and knifed along the sidewalk, a thin man with an upturned collar on his overcoat stepped inside the shop.

Abe Scholtsky heard the tinkling of the bell over the door, peered over the cover of his laptop, and shoved his glasses up to the bridge of his nose. He locked the screen, stood up, and walked around his neat desk, placing a Bic pen into a chrome holder as he stepped into the waiting room.

"Hello. I'm Abe Scholtsky, manager of Lou Cypher's Insurance Agency. Is there anything I can help you with?" Furtively, Abe glanced at the large clock directly overhead where the man had stepped inside off the street. 4:30. Hopefully, this wouldn't take long, as he was scheduled to be at the library over on 148th at 5:45.

The tall man shrugged off his overcoat, swiping his hand over his combed-back hair. He hung the coat on a rack, extended his hand, and said with a slight accent, "Yes, I'm looking to purchase a life insurance policy."

Abe studied the man, just as intently as he pored over actuarial tables and spreadsheets. He looked at the expensive but worn shoes, the creased but well-washed pants, and the matching dark suit jacket. Beneath the jacket, he wore a white shirt with a perfectly assembled Windsor knot adorning his solid red tie. His smile split his clean-shaven face evenly. His eyes were a bright blue; his nose aquiline; his eyebrows black with streaks of grey. His face was clean, a shade on the pale side, but his stance and movements were firm and confident. Abe couldn't place his age, anywhere between 45 to 65, as his hair was also lightly streaked with grey.

Abe shook his cold hand and stated, "Certainly. Would you like to come to my desk and I'll discuss the terms with you?"

The man nodded and took the proffered chair in front of Abe's desk. Abe did notice that the man glanced once back at the front door before sitting down.

Abe pulled out his swivel chair, unlocked the screen, tabbed down to life insurance quotes, opened the page and raised his eyes to the man. Immediately, he noticed the sharp canines that were protruding over the gentleman's bottom lip.

"Are you a vampire, Mr.—"

"Yes. Ulysses Frankman."

"I see. Mr. Frankman, if you are here to kill me, I will not assist you any further in applying for life insurance. Kill me now, if that is your intention."

"Truly, Mr. Scholtsky, it is not. I am here to purchase life insurance. I was told that your firm is not averse to writing policies for… unusual clients, in various stages of distress."

"Correct. What stage of distress are you in, sir?"

"The usual. Young men seeking to make their name by killing me. It becomes tedious over time, let me assure you. I seek to purchase a policy that would protect my, shall I say, existence? My life was officially ended over three hundred years ago. I need a policy that would ensure my return, should I cease to exist."

"You do realize that I am but a manager? All policies must be approved by Mr. Cypher, the owner. He makes the final decision."

"I was unaware of that but I see no reason to allow that to deter me."

"Very well. Who would you like to be your beneficiary?"

"Myself."

Abe took his fingers off the keyboard. He rubbed his chin and yanked the end of his white mustache. "I'm not an expert in vampiric lore, Mr. Frankman. I'm assuming, and, please correct me if I'm wrong, that you are anticipating your demise? And, you are banking on your inherent ability to survive, or rather, be re-animated? Thus, you want to buy a policy to insure that you 'rise' again?"

With his volcanic blue eyes flaming, Frankman vigorously nodded consent.

"I can see that the tales I heard of the perspicacity of this agency are resoundingly true. Yes, Mr. Scholtsky, I want to insure that someone will pull out the stake from my heart. For that, I am willing to buy a policy from you."

"Let me gather all the pertinent information, present your request to Mr. Cypher, and give you an answer tomorrow. Night, I presume?"

"There is one problem with your conclusion. I will be left in a semi-conscious state upon the rising of the dreaded sun. I fear my demise will occur at that time. I may not be functional tomorrow night at this time. I need to have this policy in effect tonight. I'm willing to pay you a substantial amount of gold right now. As the old song goes, 'tomorrow may be too late.'"

Abe squinted his eyes and rubbed his temple. There goes his appointment at the library. And then the finding of Mr. Cypher and obtaining his signature and approval. All to keep an ancient vampire alive. Alas, the decision was not his to make. He must bring it to Mr. Cypher.

"Very well. It will take me some time to get a hold of Mr. Cypher but I'm positive I can provide you with an answer by midnight. Can you return here at that time?"

"I am close to being omnipotent under the cloak of

darkness. No one can impede me during those hours. I shall be here promptly."

Frankman arose, crossed over to the rack, and put on his overcoat. He reached into his pocket and flipped a coin onto the desk. Abe grabbed it, fearful that it would topple over his Tiffany lamp, and held it up to the light.

The accented voice of Frankman filled the room as he silently left. "Spanish gold, from Cortez. Tell your boss that I will return with one hundred pieces to purchase the policy I so desperately desire."

Abe Scholtsky was at his desk holding a simmering cup of coffee, the fifteen-page policy lying within a brown folder upon the desk calendar. A few minutes before midnight, he noticed the lobby filling with a sparkling mist. The mist thickened, swirled and coalesced into the form of Ulysses Frankman.

"A rather inspiring entrance but why not use the door?"

"Enemies are always watching. Caution grows with longevity, my friend," replied the vampire.

Frankman was holding a cloth bag, closed with a drawstring. He sat down in the chair before the desk, keeping his overcoat on.

"I was able to contact Mr. Cypher. He has agreed to insure your life. The terms of the policy are quite standard except for these conditions."

Frankman leaned forward, a rapt eagerness in his eyes. "Proceed."

"One, the company will only insure your resurrection one time. We will delete all knowledge of your existence after we complete our part in your death. Second, we make this offer only to you, and no other members of your immediate or extended family, sanguinary or non-sanguinary. Third, we accept no responsibility in acts that you may commit after our contractual obligation is fulfilled. Finally, after our policy has been fulfilled, you have no legal recourse to bring this matter before a court of law."

Frankman chuckled. "Truly, suing you for breach of contract is not something I have ever contemplated. I accept your terms."

"Fine. Sign here. And here and once upon the last page. I've highlighted the lines requiring your signature."

With a quick flurry, Frankman signed with the Bic pen from the holder.

"One more item, Mr. Frankman. We will need to know where you will be reposing during the diurnal hours, so our contractual obligations may be enacted."

"I must be assured, Mr. Scholtsky, that the address I reveal to you is held in strictest confidence."

"You will find that this firm has existed for decades, in part because of its excellent service to its clients and its impeccable reputation for confidentiality, sir."

"Very well. I will be sleeping within a coffin upon the basement level of the old Weimar Warehouse, intersection of Farimount Avenue and 247th Street. As per our agreement, someone from your firm will be there after sundown tomorrow to remove an annoying sliver from my heart?"

"Yes. I will be there, Mr. Frankman. Now, as to our fee?"

Lifting the bag onto the desktop, Frankman loosed the drawstring. Abe removed and counted the gold doubloons, stacking them into ten piles.

"One hundred doubloons, as per our agreement. I will be returning the one you left earlier."

"No need. Keep it as a tip."

"Thank you, Mr. Frankman. Mr. Cypher told me to tell you that he appreciates you using our firm to fulfill your insurance needs."

"Just make sure you fulfill our contract. People don't live long who betray me."

Mr. Scholtsky looked levelly into the blue eyes of

Frankman. "We have no intention of not fulfilling our contract exactly as specified in the policy. Have no doubt of that, sir."

Frankman arose and dissolved into a coruscating miasma of mist. Oddly enough, like a demonic Cheshire cat, his fanged smile was the last part to drift away, which Abe thought was eerily disconcerting.

Abe Scholtsky swallowed the last bite of his ham and rye, tossed the sandwich wrapper in the trash can, pulled back on his fleece-lined gloves and grabbed the handle of the dilapidated Weimar Warehouse door. He shoved the door open and stepped inside. The ground floor was vast, with piles of wooden crates filled with remnants of green tractor parts. The noontime sun filtered through the soot-covered windows, granting a grainy glow to the interior. The winter wind whistled through several broken windows as Abe followed an aged conveyor belt towards the rear of the building. A dark doorway with dirty steps worn from countless shoe heels descended to the basement. With each hesitant step, the light dimmed until Abe reached into his overcoat pocket and pulled out his mag-light and snapped it on.

The basement level was covered with dust and spider webs. As he focused his light forward, he realized that finding a coffin amongst all the haphazardly piled crates and boxes would be an accomplishment. He began a grid pattern search, just as he did when he located hidden words in the puzzles that he loved to solve, and eliminated the front quarter of the basement floor. As he stepped out from behind a tall stack of pallets, his foot struck a body. Abe knelt, shined his beam upon the sprawled form, and inhaled in surprise.

A crossbow bolt speared completely through the young man's neck. His eyes were bulged out and his right hand was upon the shaft as if he died while trying to pull it free from his throat. Blood splatters marked the cement floor. Following the trail towards the south wall, Abe looked up. A coffin with its lid open was on top of several pallets and the blood splatters glistened in the glare of his mag-light.

Abe peered over the base of the coffin. Lying upon his back with his hands folded across his chest, reposed the skeleton of Ulysses Frankman, dressed in the same suit that he had worn at midnight. Affixed to the underside of the coffin lid was a crossbow, with the string slack and the trigger forward. An elaborate pulley system was hooked up to the crossbow and Abe realized that whoever lifted the lid would be the unlucky victim of the booby-trap, as evidenced by the dead man upon the floor.

A sharpened wooden stake, at least two feet in length, jutted forth through the fabric of Frankman's white shirt. The vertebrae of his neck were visible as they connected into the back of his skull which was elongated with slender fangs. Abe grabbed the stake with both hands, moved closer to the coffin and jerked. The point of the stake had been driven into the wood of the coffin. Abe jerked again with no success. He wiped his hands on his pants, re-grabbed the stake and began to wiggle it back and forth. After a few seconds, the stake loosened and, with a mighty heave, he withdrew the stake from the vampire's chest.

Instantly, a glow burst outward from the empty suit. Dust rose from the bottom of the coffin box and swirled inside the skeleton. The dust motes solidified and formed into sinew and flesh which wrapped around the white bones. The suit puffed out and the features of the skull filled with cartilage and muscle. The eyes snapped open, blazing red with demonic intensity. Abe stepped back, mouth agape, with every instinct he possessed screaming at him to flee.

Frankman lunged out of the coffin, stared at the frightened man, and latched his gaunt hand around Abe's neck. Effortlessly lifting him in the air, he dropped Abe. Abe crumpled to the floor and began a crab crawl away from the vampire. Frankman blinked his eyes and the crimson ebbed into an icy blue.

"Stay away from me! Remember our agreement!" shouted Scholtsky.

Frankman stepped towards Scholtsky, baring his fangs.

"Yes. I remember it. And I am glad you have kept your end of the contract. Unfortunately, the contract is now null and void. And, my dear Mr. Scholtsky, I hunger!"

"Stop! You can't feed on me. You signed a contract!"

Frankman reached down, grabbed Scholtsky by the front of his overcoat, and lifted him to his face. The vampire reared his head back, extended his mouth like a wolf, and broke his two upper canines upon the impenetrable skin of Scholtsky.

With a howl of unaccustomed pain, he flung Scholtsky to the debris cluttered floor. His hand felt his blunted fangs and he snarled.

"Who are you?"

"It's not who am I. It is rather who do I work for?"

Abe Scholtsky stood up, holding an upside-down crucifix in his hand. Frankman stepped back, averting his face with his left arm.

In a commanding tone, Scholtsky spoke.

"Vampire, who do I work for?"

"You work for an insurance agency!"

"Yes! I work for Lou Cypher!"

And with those words, Scholtsky saw the fear of recognition flit across the face of Frankman.

"NO! What could he want from me?"

"Just your shriveled and evil soul!"

With a furious movement of his hands in an arcane pattern, the air became humid, banishing the winter chill. A Sulphur stench filled the air. A jagged rupture appeared before the vampire and a clawed hand stretched forth, enveloping Frankman like a vulture's talon clutching a decaying rat.

"Forgive me, great one! Forgive me, LUCIPHER."

And with a resounding clap of thunder, the hand whisked the vampire into its fiery realm.

Abe Scholtsky gingerly touched his neck and leaned back into his plush office chair. He drank a long slug of coffee and dusted from his desktop into his cupped hand a few crumbs from his ham and rye. Tossing the crumbs into his wastebasket, he adjusted his glasses and re-read his e-mail to his boss, Lou Cypher. Satisfied that his letter covered all the salient points concerning the Frankman policy, he hit the send icon. Reaching out, he hefted the fifteen-page policy and turned to page 9, paragraph 5, double ii. "In the event of early termination or unauthorized rescindment of the policy by the insured, severe penalties may be imposed by the company."

He shook his head in dismay, once again astounded by the number of clients who never read the entire policy and willfully sign page fifteen without ever realizing what they have endorsed.

Oh well, that's why the Lou Cypher Insurance Agency has been in business for millennia, far longer than those upstart vampires who think that a few centuries of existence places them on a level with his boss. He smiled smugly and took another long sip from his cup.

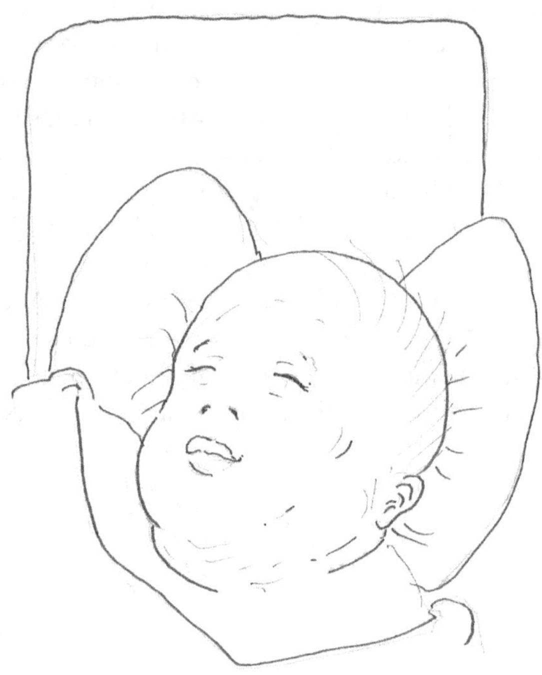

"He has his father's dark hair and complexion," a fifty-ish
woman commented.

Hot Out Of The Oven

By Jeffrey Vavra

Holding the phone to her ear, Miranda cradled her burgeoning stomach in her right hand. "Yes, I'm going to deliver today. I have a midwife in the family who will help me. Hopefully, it will all be over before I know what happened." She laughed then listened for a moment. "I appreciate the offer but I have several relatives in town and friends over today who can help." She listened some more. "Okay, bye-bye."

"Just the neighbor asking if I needed anything," Miranda said to the group of women seated around her. "It would have been rude not to take the call with all the people she has seen coming and going in the last two days."

"We're pretty much ready when you are, dear." A woman in her middle fifties wearing tie-dyed hospital scrubs came up to Miranda. "The bedroom has been prepared. I put a plastic sheet on to protect the mattress, and I brought some disposable linen so you don't have to dirty any of your own. There are extra towels, sterile water to wash the baby, and a mild tranquilizer if needed. Speaking of which, would you like a relaxant?" the midwife asked.

Miranda laughed and picked up her glass of champagne. "I don't suppose you were talking about more of this were you, Lacey?"

"I was thinking more in the lines of a nice herbal tea." Lacey laughed with the others.

One of Miranda's girlfriends, Abbey, a petite woman with short, spiky blonde hair winked at Miranda and motioned with her eyes to the coffee table in front of them. "Sooo," she said. "Presents now or after the birth?"

Miranda looked at the coffee table filled with brightly wrapped boxes and cheery gift bags brought for the occasion. "They are beautiful. Could I open them now? Maybe I'll get a gift of courage like the Cowardly Lion in The Wizard of Oz."

"Don't be silly," Abbey said, putting a hand on Miranda's leg as she sat next to her on the couch. "You are going to be just fine. You've got Lacey. She's delivered the first baby for every mother in this room. Here, open mine first." Abbey fished a blue box out of the pile and handed it to Miranda.

Miranda untied the ribbon and opened the box, pulling the tissue paper aside. "A gift certificate to Maggie's Salon and Spa," she said, "how thoughtful."

"You'll have plenty of time to pamper yourself after you deliver. A massage, facial, manicure, and pedicure are included."

"That's so where I want to be right now." Miranda leaned over as far as she could to hug Abbey. She giggled as the two bumped stomachs. "You're going to have to meet me more than halfway," she told Abbey.

Miranda pulled another gift from the pile. This time a blue bag covered with glitter. She reached inside and pulled out a package of cotton pads and a box of tea. "Sage," she said, holding it up for everybody to see.

"You may lactate a bit after giving birth until your milk dries up," Lacey said. "The tea can help the process along a bit faster. The pads go in your bra to absorb the milk."

"You think of everything."

Lacey smiled. "So you don't have to," she said.

"What's Stephen up to?" Miranda asked, looking around.

"He's opening some gifts from the men," Nadia, a slim brunette, said while walking into the room. "I think he just unwrapped a subscription to a men's magazine or something and a dating form for a singles matchmaking service. Mostly gag gifts from what I could see when I poked my head inside the den. Nothing practical like you're getting."

"Oh, yeah, edible panties, practical," Miranda said, holding up a purple pair she had just pulled from a pink bag with white ribbons. This brought shrieks of laughter from the other women.

"Wow, you girls are certainly having a great time in here."

They all turned. "Hey, there's the other half," someone said.

"I hear you've been getting some racy gifts," Miranda said.

"They'll keep me busy, no doubt about that. I didn't want to interrupt. I just came for some extra wine glasses. Where do you keep them? Oh, and some napkins."

"The glasses are in the cupboard next to the refrigerator," Miranda said.

"Ah-yes, great, thanks a lot."

"If the napkins are gone from the counter next to the coffee maker, there are more in the pantry."

"And the pantry is where?" Stephen asked looking around.

"I'll show him," Abbey said, jumping up from the sofa.

The rest of the women turned back to the table of gifts and in a matter of thirty minutes, Miranda had opened each present. Some were whimsical in nature, such as perfume and lingerie, while others were inducements to lose the pregnancy weight with bikinis and day trips and a gift certificate with the personal trainer—who they all agreed was handsome and eligible—at a local gym where several of the women had memberships.

Standing up, Miranda announced: "I've put off the inevitable long enough. Lacey, shall we?" she said, and held her hand out for her midwife.

Miranda gave each of the five women a hug and received in return encouragement, well wishes, and promises that everything will go quickly and smoothly.

She then took Lacey's arm and waddled off in the direction of the bedroom, leaving the others to tell the men the ceremony had begun.

Three hours later a tall, well-dressed man in his late fifties wearing an exquisitely tailored black suit entered Miranda's bedroom. With his white hair, pearl-white teeth and darkly tanned skin, he was the very picture of everyone's favorite grandfather. "Things went well I hope," Ambrose said addressing Lacey.

"Very well, indeed. There were no complications."

"Here it is, hot out of the oven." Lacey let a giggle slip, for she loved to use the traditional phrases such as "nothing says lovin' like a bun in the oven." Lacey picked up the child—a boy—wrapped in white sackcloth and passed him to a stern-looking woman who had come in with the tall man, who then took the child and exited the bedroom.

With his back to Miranda, Ambrose whispered to Lacey, "I can count on you to take care of getting the afterbirth to the appropriate person?"

"Of course, yes," she replied.

The tall man walked up to the side of the bed and took Miranda's hand in his tanned one. "I hear you did splendidly.

The baby is healthy. You and Stephen have done a remarkable job."

"Thank you, Ambrose." Miranda spoke quietly, the painkillers made her drowsy.

"You just sleep a bit," he said, "and we'll talk again later. I'm going to congratulate Stephen."

The dining room had been prepared for a sumptuous meal. A white linen tablecloth adorned a long table complete with elaborate place settings dotting the circumference. Fine china and silverware were set in a formal pattern that included a finger bowl for each participant. Three silver stick candelabra placed an equal distance from each other on the table burned white tapers. A half dozen bottles of red wine sat on a serving cart off to the side.

"Ah, and here's the cook now," Ambrose said, as he saw Miranda pushed into the dining room in a wheelchair.

"Compliments to the chef," they all said and raised their glasses in salute.

"How are you feeling, dear?"

"Surprisingly, quite good. Lacey's potions are still working their magic."

"Fabulous. Lacey, if you would help Miranda to her place, please."

Lacey pushed the wheelchair to the opposite end of the table and installed Miranda alongside Stephen at the head of the table.

Ambrose stood. "We are here today to celebrate Miranda and Stephen's unselfish act of bringing another soul into this world to be shared by us all."

The table toasted Miranda and Stephen.

Two medium-sized, white china bowls were wheeled in on a serving cart. In each was a reddish chowder mixture with white chunks. The same tall woman that had taken the child from Lacey in Miranda's bedroom ladled a portion into a bowl in front of each person as she circled the table pushing the cart. When all were served, Ambrose gestured to Stephen and Miranda with an open hand that they were to begin.

"As is our custom the parents of the child will start us off. With this first bite the union that began almost ten months ago is dissolved," Ambrose said and sat down.

Both Miranda and Stephen took up their soup spoons from their place on the table. Miranda dipped hers into the bowl on her plate, gently stirred the white and blood-red mixture of tissue, and ate.

Ambrose followed Miranda and Stephen, who was then eagerly followed by the others at the table. "Delicious," he said.

The door to the kitchen pushed in and the tall woman from before came in and handed the naked infant to Ambrose.

Ambrose stood and held the squirming infant out so everyone could get a better look.

"He has his father's dark hair and complexion," a fifty-ish woman commented.

"The eyes are dark," commented another. A good omen they all agreed.

Ambrose handed the baby off to the tall woman who placed the now crying infant on a silver oval serving platter. She then carried the platter and its occupant around the table and set it in front of Miranda and Stephen.

"I now bring this meeting to order with the arrival of the sacrifice." Ambrose unwrapped a large, ornate carving knife with a highly polished silver blade from a sleeve of white silk, and passed it down to Stephen and Miranda.

"Let us begin," Miranda said, as she held the baby's head, while both she and Stephen held the knife like any married couple would about to carve their wedding cake.

Abbey looked down and rubbed the bump at her waist and smiled.

Sprawled upon the floor of the elevator, grass tufting up through its legs and its tail nervously twitching, was an alligator.

The Elevator

By Rex Munsee

    I'm the janitor at the Johnson County Courthouse. I live in a two-room apartment behind the bowling alley on Eucalyptus Street, a borough of Johnsonburg. I've gotten used to the sound of bouncing pins and clunking bowling balls. Every Monday through Friday I walk six blocks to the back door of the courthouse, unlock it, pull out my floor duster, and do what I've done for the last 45 years. Am I sick of it? Yes. Does it pay the bills? Just barely.

    Although I am tired of the constant upkeep—the never-ending mopping of melted snow during the endless Pennsylvania winters, the cleaning of brittle leaves out of the eaves and drains, the months of pushing a John Deere mower—I am proud of the building. Constructed in 1832, it has old mahogany staircases that sweep from the front lobby up to the main courtroom on the second floor, and gain up to the third floor which houses the Veterans Affairs office and the Domestic Relations offices. The courtroom has a 20-foot tall ceiling that is made of tongue-in-groove cherry boards with varnished wainscoting that runs 4 feet up the wall until it melts into a chair rail. From the rail to the ceiling is old plaster, protected by high-gloss eggshell colored paint. I should know, I painted it with a roller and an 18-foot ladder. Judge Scott was so pleased with it that he took me out for a steak dinner.

Marble protects the walls on the first, second, and third floors. The floor is an intricately-laid tile of a green and sapphire design. The old wood and coal furnace was removed back in 1947 when they made the basement into office spaces. A natural gas furnace took its place, keeping the water hot as it spits and thumps through the pipes and radiators, like the blood pulsing through the arteries of a living person. The rear of the building was sacrificed to the Americans with Disabilities Act in 1977, and the beautiful staircase, identical to the front, was torn out and an elevator was installed. They put in a cement staircase but it has none of the character of the old one; it's functional, that's all I'll say good about it except it did open up the building to vets with wooden legs and old people in wheelchairs. It's just not intrinsic to the building, kind of like putting a pacemaker on the outside of your chest.

The only other architecturally striking feature of the courthouse is the clock tower. It rises 50 feet high from the front side of the building, adjacent to Main Street. The clock still runs as I keep the precision machinery that powers the four clocks on all sides in order. On top of the clock roof is a statue of Lady Liberty, holding her scales of justice. Ironically enough, when the exterior of the courthouse was refurbished back in '03, there were several bullet holes in Lady L. Not everyone agrees with the jurors' verdicts, I suppose. The only other things that Lady L. attracts are many bolts of lightning, especially during the thunderstorms of July and August. It is a certainty that at least once a year, I will be replacing slagged breaker switches, and the commissioners of Johnson County will be scrambling to find money to pay electricians for installing new wiring and computers.

Lightning striking clock towers is not surprising. However, what happened to me last Friday night is beyond surprising. Let me explain. Judge Scott was presiding over a jury trial. A guy named William Stango had been charged with molesting his step-daughter over a period of years. The cops had found pictures of the 11 year-old girl, nude, and being molested, on Stango's computer. However, all anyone could see of the rapist was his dick. The cops charged Stango with a host of sex crimes. Stango denied them. Thus, a trial to prove he was guilty. The whole case rested on the girl's testimony. And here's where it got worse – she was mildly mentally handicapped. Not a slack-jawed drooler but her mind wandered easily. The District Attorney, Reginal Simmons, was having difficulty getting her to understand and focus on his questions. I snuck in to watch the closing arguments. The Defense was old smoothie Tommy Colorado. In his 600 buck suit, with his gray hair slicked back, and his tongue glibly portraying the holes in the girl's testimony to the jury, even I had doubts. Simmons fired back, stressing the pictures were on Stango's computer and he had access to the girl. I could hear the anguish in Simmons's voice – he was worried Stango was gonna walk free.

Judge Scott charged the jury and they filed out to the third-floor deliberation room to mull the case over. I knew it would take some time so I slipped down the two flights of stairs and walked over to the sub shop. The muggy July evening was brewing into a storm. The wind held the smell of rain and all the leaves on the trees in the park were turning upwards. Towards the horizon, the clouds were scuttling and darkening. I ate a meatball sub, drank a Dr. Pepper, and debated whether to walk home and finish cleaning the courtroom on Saturday morning. I decided that I'd rather sleep in or hike down over to the river and fish, so I walked back to the courthouse. The clock tower showed 7:10.

Simmons was standing at the bottom of the steps, smoking a Camel. He had loosened his tie in the heat and I could see sweat stains around his white shirt collar.

"Christ, Reggie, the last time I saw a black man sweating like that outside the courthouse, some Klansmen were holding a noose."

"Fuck you, Clarence. Those Klansmen were probably all your kin, as your white ass family tree has no branches."

We both smiled and he inhaled on his cigarette.

"No word yet from the jury?"

"Not a peep. Moving into the second hour now. I wish I could hear what's going on inside that room."

"Well, he did it in my book. Hope you convict that bastard."

"Me, too."

"Hey, I'm hanging around to clean up after. My office is open and I've got the AC running if you need a place to relax."

"Okay, I'll be down later. My office is just too far from the courthouse."

I unlocked the door to my office, hit the remote, and flicked the TV onto a hunting channel. The window AC unit had it cooled down to a refreshing 69 degrees. I opened my cubicle refrigerator and unscrewed the top off of another Dr. Pepper. My feet were propped up on the desktop, my hands were folded over my chest, and I was slouched back in my swivel chair, half-asleep, when a crack of lightning exploded outside.

I jumped up, opened my door and started walking down the empty basement floor towards the elevator. I was 10 feet from it when the double doors slid open on their own. Inside, the elevator glowed a deep red and an aroma of a muck-filled swamp wafted out. I stopped and stared. Sprawled upon the floor of the elevator, grass tufting up through its legs and its tail nervously twitching, was an alligator.

I froze. The double doors shut, and I could hear the

elevator rising. I ran to the stairs and vaulted them two at a time, reaching the first floor almost as soon as the elevator. I rounded the corner and the double doors were still shut. I punched the button and stepped back. When the doors slid back, all that was inside was a white interior, red carpet, and a list of emergency instructions. Gingerly, I stuck my head inside. No alligator. No grass. No swamp smell. I stepped back and collapsed on an inside bench. The double doors shut.

I wiped the sweat from my brow. I'm not an alcoholic. I'm not on any kind of medicine. I've never had hallucinations before. Why the hell did I see an alligator in a swamp in the elevator? I continued up to the second floor, where the courtroom was located. As I pushed open the swinging doors to the corridor, I could see the Judge's secretary, Brenda, inside at her desk. Standing in the hall was the bailiff, Derek Cooper. He glanced at me and nodded. Then he looked at me again.

"Are you all right, Clarence? You look pale."

"I'm okay. That last bolt of lightning just startled me a bit. Jury still out?"

"Yep. I think they're just waiting for the Judge to order them supper. KFC on the county's dime."

The red light shone above the double black elevator door. Derek was standing with his back to the doors as they opened. From inside, Atty. Colorado stepped out.

"Hey, Derek, have you seen DA Simmons? The Judge wants the both of us in chambers."

"I'll have Brenda dial his cell." Derek pivoted and walked towards Brenda's office.

I craned my neck and could only see the normal interior of the elevator as the double doors shut.

"I'll check downstairs for him," I said to no one in particular. As I made my way down the back steps, I looked out the long windows that light up the rear wall. It was raining hard and I could hear rumblings of thunder but no streaks of lightning were flashing. Good. Maybe the worst of this storm had passed by.

As I stepped out onto the tile floor of the basement, I saw Reginal coming from the direction of my office, his cell to his ear. He nodded, punched the button to the elevator, waited briefly, and stepped inside the fluorescent-lit box. No alligator was waiting for him. I unlocked my office door, took another swallow of Dr. Pepper, and settled back in my chair.

I awakened to the sound of someone pounding on my door. My digital clock showed 8:15. I opened the door and Reggie walked in, holding a plastic bag filled with a sub.

"Sit on down. I've got stuff to drink in the fridge."

He looked at me with a half-smile on his face. "I don't want just Coke."

"Counselor, you know it would be breaking Johnson County rules to drink liquor on County property," I said as I reached into my toolbox, removed the top tray, and pulled out a metal flask. I poured some of the rum into his cup of Coke. Tipped some more of it into my Dr. Pepper bottle, and we bumped our containers together. After we each drained a healthy slug, he replied, "Of course, it would also be against the ethics of the bar to drink while engaged in a trial."

"Has it quit raining?"

"Yeah, but the humidity is rising again. I think another storm is still brewing. Let me check."

He pulled out his cell, punched a button, and shook his head. "Yep, another line of storms is heading in from Ohio, and they're all colored red, according to this channel."

"Still no verdict?"

"No. You'd think on a Friday night the jurors would have some other plans on their minds rather than staying here and eating greasy chicken. But what can you expect? None of them were smart enough to get out of jury duty. When you throw together twelve people of average ignorance, anything can happen."

I poured more rum into my Dr. Pepper but Reggie shook his head "No." "Christ, Clarence, I can't take too big of a chance."

"Yeah, your job's important. Me, I'm just the janitor." And I took another big slug from my bottle.

Reggie stayed and watched TV for almost an hour. I finished off my rum and was feeling a nice mellow buzz running through my brain. Before I could stop myself, I blurted out what I had seen on the elevator.

Reggie looked at me. "You sure you hadn't been hitting the bottle already?"

"No. At that time, I was sober as Judge Scott."

"Well, if we eliminate that you were drunk and that you're not lying, my guess is it was because of the lightning."

"Come again?" I leaned closer to him from across my desk.

"Lightning is powerful, right up there with tornadoes and hurricanes. But where they hit large areas, lightning concentrates in one specific location. Just suppose that bolt hit the tower and it funneled down the elevator and when it grounded out, it blasted an opening into another dimension or allowed another space/time continuum to leach over into our world. That could account for what you saw."

"You are crazy, my friend."

"Hey, I'm not the one seeing alligators in elevators."

"Point taken. But there's no…"

Reggie's cell phone buzzed. He grabbed it, spoke, and started getting up. "We've got a verdict."

Reggie stood up, straightened his blue tie, and left my office. I walked to the far end of the hall, stepped into the Men's Room, and relieved myself into a full-length porcelain urinal. Try finding those beauties in a modern building. I washed my face and hands. As I exited, I stopped at the drinking fountain and swallowed some cold water. I could hear rain pummeling the windows and the crack of a lightning bolt striking. As I stepped down the hallway towards the elevator, the doors opened.

Standing inside, beneath the glow of a smoky red light, was a shaggy caveman. He was half-crouched, long arms akimbo, glaring at me with his beady eyes. In his right hand was a spear. Surrounding his feet were green ferns and sandy soil. As he pulled his arm back to hurtle the spear, a tawny-colored saber-toothed tiger pounced onto his back. The cat screamed and the caveman yelled in fear as he went down, his muscled back spurting gouts of red blood from the cat's raking claws. Then the double doors slid shut.

I ran to the doors and hit the red button. The light showed "Up." I heard the sound of the car being lifted up the shaft. The noise quieted and I knew the car was on the first floor. The light showed "Down." I slipped around the corner, with my back to the storage room. The car hummed to a stop, a bell chimed, and the doors slid open. I peeked around the corner and the interior of the elevator was as normal as a Rockwell painting. No blood splashed on the wall, no ferns, no saber-toothed tigers nor shaggy caveman. I hit the button again and, after a pause, the double doors slid shut and the elevator car ascended.

I scrambled up the steps until I stopped on the second floor. I paused to catch my breath as I stepped off the carpeted steps onto the tile mosaic which made up the lobby floor. I pushed open the large door and quickly slipped into the side back pew. Deputy Zimmerman was sitting in the swivel chair to my left. He nodded at me as I looked over my shoulder at him.

"You made it just in time," he whispered.

Straight ahead, Bailiff Cooper was standing behind his desk, which was just below the judge's bench. To his right was the vice-prothonotary, a slender lady who administered all the oaths to the witnesses and marked all the evidentiary exhibits into their proper order. Next to the now empty witness chair was the court stenographer, Belinda Nichols, who was wearing a blue dress and double-checking the accuracy of her transcript.

With their backs to me, sitting behind a long wooden table with a glass top, were DA Simmons, the arresting officer, and Asst. D.A. Tamara Wilford. Down three empty chairs sat the defendant, William Stango, in a black suit with his hair pulled back into a ponytail, and next to him, in a splendid suit of dark green was the silver-tongued devil, Atty. Tommy Colorado. The side door pushed open and an elderly man named Wilbert Reynolds, the tipstaff, walked slowly in, leaning heavily on his cane. Behind him in single file walked the jury. As they filed past the attorneys and the defendant, they climbed into the jury stand and stood before their chairs.

"All rise!" stated Bailiff Cooper, "the honorable Judge Lester Scott is upon the bench."

"Be seated," Judge Scott said amiably, appearing from his chamber door behind his bench. His voice was interrupted by the slashing of rain against the south wall of windows in the courtroom.

I watched the storm, paying more attention to its fury—the whistling and gusting winds, the low rumble of thunder, the streaks of lightning pulsing through the darkened sky—than I did the wordplay between the judge and the jury foreman. When I glanced to the bench, the jury foreman was just beginning to read the verdict.

"In the matter of the Commonwealth of Pennsylvania versus William Stango, we the jury find to the first count of Rape, Not Guilty. To the second charge of Involuntary Deviant Intercourse, Not Guilty. To the third charge of Statutory Rape,

Not Guilty. To the fourth charge of Indecent Assault, Not Guilty. To the last charge of Corruption of Minors, Not Guilty."

Stango reached out and grabbed his attorney around his shoulders. I noticed the slumping of Simmons's shoulders for a few seconds and then he lifted them back up. It was a hard pill to swallow, but he couldn't allow himself to show any emotion. He had done his job and lost. The only sound I could hear was from the family of the 11 year-old girl. They were in the pews hugging and sobbing in strangled, low gasps.

Judge Scott thanked the jurors for their service, advised them to return their yellow "Jury" buttons to Mr. Reynolds, and declared the court was adjourned. He slid through the narrow door behind his chair and into his chambers.

I stood up, nodded to Deputy Zimmerman, pushed open the door, entered the lobby, and descended the three flights to the basement of the courthouse. I unlocked my office, decided to give everyone ten minutes to clear out, and then start cleaning up the courtroom. It was quiet in my office, all I could hear was the storm raging outside, and I was about to click on my TV when I heard the loud sound of boots clunking down the steps. I cracked open the door and saw William Stango enter into the Men's Room.

Shit, I thought. Now I'll have to clean that stall again.

I grabbed my cart, which held my vacuum cleaner, brooms, cleaners and rags. I pushed them towards the elevator. I kept remembering the spooky images I had seen earlier and decided to wait until Stango left the restroom before cleaning up his mess. Then I would drag the vacuum cleaner up the steps to the courtroom.

I heard the toilet flush. I leaned against the tiled wall and adjusted my cleaning supplies. I could hear a man's voice speaking loudly into a cell phone, "Yeah, no one believed that retard. I'm a free man, baby! I'll see you in just a few minutes."

He burst out of the restroom and headed to the stairs. And that is when I made up my mind.

"Sir?" I said in a weak voice. "Sir?"

He stopped and looked at me. "What!"

"I just mopped the stairs. They're all wet. Could you please use the elevator?"

He puffed up his chest, glared at me with a scowl, and walked back towards me.

"You're lucky I'm in a good mood, pal. What are you, the fucking janitor?"

"Yes, I am," I said, cowering back towards the restroom door.

He stabbed the button with his finger. I could hear thunder and the crack of lightning. The light flared and I could hear the sound of the car descending. The bell rang. The double doors slid open. Stango stepped back, his mouth agape. I lowered my head and charged him, shoving him into the car. I saw him trip over the back of an alligator and saw the alligator's tail whip back and forth. I heard a scream and the sound of cracking bones as the alligator lunged forward. I reached out, shoved the button, and ran back down the hallway. I never looked back and bolted up the front steps to the first floor. I crossed down the large lobby and went to the elevator. I hit the button. The doors slid open. Inside was nothing. No alligator. No man. Just the clean interior of an old elevator.

I walked back to the basement. I put away all my cleaning supplies and locked up my office. I walked out the back doors of the courthouse and hurried to my apartment six blocks away. I was soaked by the time I arrived. For some reason, I felt cleaner than I had in years.

He likened it to a display case in a butcher shop where you walk the cases comparing the size and cuts of meat, the cost of taking it, and the amount of satisfaction bringing it home will give you.

The Meat Market

By Jeffrey Vavra

"Jees, Carter, about time you got here," Taylor said. The speaker was in his mid-thirties and dressed business casual, a contrast to the relaxed atmosphere of the festive palm fronds, miniature waterfalls, and waiters and waitresses dressed in Hawaiian costume. Even the bamboo chair he sat in reflected the tropical theme of the bar's outdoor patio.

"Got that right," the blond-haired man agreed as he walked up to the table. Like his partner, Carter was also in his mid-thirties and well dressed in grey pleated slacks, a tie and white shirt. "Getting the van detailed took longer than I thought. This one was way over on the east side of town."

That's what Taylor liked about his mentor, his attention to detail. Cleaned at a different place each time, a dirty van is something that could come back to bite them in the ass. Taylor stated the obvious: "It won't be long before we'll need to make a trade for another model."

Carter put the light beer he bought on his way past the outdoor bar down on the table and pulled out the chair. "Have you been busy prospecting?" he said, not worried about who heard him. "Any front runners?"

"At this stage, they're all pretty much just prospects. There's a good mix that shuffles through here though."

Carter smiled. "We've got time. We don't want to rush into anything until we're ready again. At least not without the proper sign." He sat down and quickly scanned the crowd of mostly young office drones milling about. Dressed similarly, drinking similar beer the two blended in easily with the office types. He loosened his purple tie with one hand and picked up his beer with the other. Ignoring the prospects, he settled back and looked up into the sky. "Have you looked to the clouds?"

"The what?" his accomplice asked, distracted by a young woman seated at the table near them. She was—what was the term—big-boned. Sturdy. A nice change he thought from the anorexic figure of the last one. Taylor took his cell phone out and took her picture without her noticing. He fingered the knife on the table he had earlier undressed from the blood-red napkin. He manipulated the cool stainless steel instrument through his fingers with a surgeon's familiarity. The weight and shape reminded him of a No. 3 scalpel.

"The clouds, the clouds up in the sky," Carter repeated, as he watched them meander by.

Taylor turned from the picture of the young woman he captured on his phone to his friend, then up to the bright blue sky, only to frown. The clouds reminded him of the smoke rings his father pushed in his face from his cigar when he was a boy.

"Only to check the weather," Taylor finally said. He put the knife down and picked up the napkin to dab at the condensation that fell from his bottle of import beer onto his dress pants. He then wrapped it around the base of the bottle while he looked with a discerning eye on the after-work throngs moving back and forth in front of him. He likened it to a display case in a butcher shop where you walk the cases comparing the size and cuts of meat, the cost of taking it, and the amount of satisfaction bringing it home will give you.

Carter continued to stare up above their heads. "You

ever think that certain clouds look like certain people?" he asked, taking a long swallow of his beer.

It always started the same way. Like a nightclub routine they performed before an audience Friday and Saturday nights and twice on Sunday.

"Like that one there," he said, pointing up in the air.

Taylor didn't look.

"That looks like Ms. Fisher the BMW salesman—woman," he added quickly, correcting himself, "with her big eyes. Remember her? That one looks like…ah, what was her name, the hostess at that make-out bar. Wendy, wasn't it?" He imagined he saw the soft curves of her hourglass figure prominent in the rolling mass of fluffy white, and let himself relive the memories and felt the warmth spread throughout his limbs.

"What? Wendy, right," Taylor said. His eyes jumped noncommittally from person to person, table to table. He was lost in his thoughts comparing one prospect to another, sometimes to a former prospect. Would she hold up as well or better than the others, he wondered. Would she just give up or prolong the sport by fighting back? He had picked up the knife again. His thumb moved back and forth in a sawing motion over the sharp edge. But never hard enough to break the skin. He knew how much pressure to apply before the skin separated. He brought it up to his mouth and drew it across his tongue, cutting it, and tasted blood.

"They're like Rorschach drawings," Carter said.

"Hmmm?"

"The clouds are like Rorschach drawings," Carter explained. "The inkblots. Psyches use them to help define your personality depending on what you see in that…well, blot."

Taylor turned around quickly in his chair. His voice was low. "When did you start going to a psychiatrist?" There was panic in his voice.

"I'm not. I've just read about it. I think about it now every time I see someone in the clouds."

"You and your clouds. I get it that you see things in the clouds. But this idea that they influence your life—my life…" Taylor didn't finish. Carter couldn't make a decision without consulting the clouds like they were some Oracle of Delphi. The clouds that dictated their choices. The clouds that told him when to get started. The clouds that told him where they would do it. The clouds that told him who they did.

"Some people say the same thing about the stars—that they influence your life, I mean. But clouds, they speak to me. They show me things."

"Well, that bartender speaks to me," Taylor said, having moved from the woman at the adjacent table to the female mixing drinks behind the bar. He brought up his phone again and unobtrusively snapped her picture.

Carter turned his blue eyes from the sky to glance over his left shoulder to the bar. "Long or short hair?"

"Short."

Carter took a moment to study the dark-haired bartender, her head encircled with a wreath of pink carnations, her Hawaiian shirt pulled up high and knotted under her breasts in a farmer's daughter kind of way. Around her neck was a lei of silk flowers of various sizes and shapes and colors and patterns not found in nature. Carter went back to the sky.

"Well?" Taylor asked.

Carter said nothing. When he got around to it, Carter was going to say no. Taylor knew it. His prospects are rarely approved. Too old too young too big too small too dangerous too much like the last one. What was it Carter said? Diversity. Diversity provides opportunity. You don't want to become predictable—go to the well too often. He understood the logic of that. Patterns were traceable. Still, he wished his prospects were considered.

Taylor knew better than to interrupt Carter right now. He was lost in the sky. So Taylor waited and went back to watching the parade of prospects going by, scrutinizing, evaluating. He watched the prospects interact with one another, raising their glasses in toasts, laughing. He imagined the office gossip they were exchanging. He's sleeping with her? Who got what promotion? The client is guilty of what? Can you believe she said that?

Not taking his eyes from the sky, as if reading a script printed on a cloud, Carter spoke.

"I think she has promise and bears closer watching." He brought his eyes down, put the beer bottle on the table, and turned his chair a bit so he could comfortably watch the bar without looking like he was watching her.

Taylor smiled, raised his beer to his partner, and turned his chair just a bit himself and snapped another picture.

I was intrigued as to what kind of problem a Central County cop like me could solve for him.

Fallen Light

By Rex Munsee

I heard the buzz of my cell phone, put down my book, glanced at the number on the screen, saw that it wasn't the number for the station, and pressed the talk button.

"Mitch?" A male voice said hesitantly. "This is Ron Arrent."

"Yeah, Ron. This is Mitch. What can I do for you?"

"Sorry to bother you at home and when it's late…but I've got a problem."

The digital clock on the stand by my easy chair showed 10:45.

"That's all right. I take an unmarked car home every night just in case I get called out. I'm just sitting here reading. Is everything all right with Janey and the kids?"

Ron Arrent is a buddy of mine who lives five miles down the state highway in a little town called North Nineveh. He and his wife and kids go to the same church I do. When we bump into each other at the grocery store, we swap hunting stories. A good guy who causes no one any trouble. I was intrigued as to what kind of problem a Central County cop like me could solve for him.

"Mitch, my older brother Sam, who lives out in Ohio, called me this morning. His wife of 48 years, Sarah, has been having…mental problems. She's been on medicine for years.

Just of late, she has sworn off her pills. She's been getting delusional. She thinks Sam is an impostor. She talks to God and has become zealously religious. Her two daughters have tried to help her but she refuses to go to a doctor or start back up on her pills. She claims it interferes with her "hearing" of God's words."

"Sam called me at noon today. He said that when he got home from going to the post office this morning, Sarah was gone in their green Toyota. She wouldn't answer her phone. He's scared she's run off on some mission. He reported her missing to the county sheriff."

"About half an hour ago, there was a knock on my door. Janey answered it and there stood Sarah. We let her in and she's going to spend the night here. She's kooky but fairly normal. We're in no danger from her but I'm worried how she will react when Sam gets here in the morning. I've already called him. He wants to get her some help in the psych center. I know there is going to be a big scene. Can you be here then? We may need you to transport her to the hospital if she refuses to go."

"What time will your brother be at your house?"

"By the time he leaves Ohio, drives across I-80, and winds his way down these curvy PA roads, it'll be at least 4 in the morning."

"Give me a call around 7:30. I'll call in to the station and adjust my schedule. I'll be down then. Maybe this will all go pretty smooth."

"I hope so. This has been real hard on Sam."

Before I hung up, I had him give me Sam's number. I told Ron not to worry and to call me if anything happened during the night.

I called Sam Arrent. He answered on the third ring. His voice was tired. I told him who I was and he re-told the story his brother had just given me. I found out that Sarah had been on depression medicine for years and had once before got so bad that she had driven away, but she had returned unharmed. A new doctor had changed her meds and things had been copacetic for years. Sarah was 65, a mother of two married daughters, a secretary at the Baptist Church, and now she was communicating with God. She had argued with Sam and their daughters about her needing to take her medicines. She felt there was nothing wrong with her that Jesus couldn't heal.

I told him I'd see him in the morning and to drive carefully.

"Mr. Remmings, what happens if Sarah won't voluntarily commit herself to the psych hospital?"

"Well, in PA, she would have to be evaluated by a mental health delegate. If they find her a danger to herself or others, they can commit her against her will."

There was a long pause. "I'm afraid it may come to that. She is firmly against taking any medications."

I woke up at 6:30. I did my triple S's in the bathroom and went downstairs to drink a cup of coffee. The automatic brewer was done and I poured a dark blend into a Styrofoam cup. I uncapped the tube of anti-itching cream for my poison ivy that I'd caught last weekend while chainsawing firewood out back. Doc Williams had prescribed it for me over the phone and it was providing some relief from the red scratches on the back of my right hand and wrist. Even with the cream, I still woke up itching in the middle of the night.

I drank the black coffee, crumpled the cup, tossed it into the garbage can, and walked outside into a foggy August morning. The dew covered all of my flowers and shrubs and I could smell the crispness in the air. I unlocked my Crown Victoria, swiped the wiper blades against the wet windshield, and turned the defroster on. I called in to dispatch and told them I was en route to North Nineveh. Out of habit, I patted my holster beneath my tan suit jacket, felt the hard outline of my .45 Glock, and adjusted my seatbelt.

Fifteen minutes later, I pulled into Ron Arrent's driveway which runs parallel to his three-story house. Ahead of me was parked his Chevy pickup, Janey's VW Jetta, and a Toyota with Ohio plates. I radioed in my location, got out, scratched my right hand until I could feel fresh blood, grimaced, and walked onto the covered front porch. I knocked and Janey opened the door, dressed in a robe and slippers.

"Morning, Mitch. Come on in. The men are in the kitchen. Sarah's still upstairs sleeping."

We passed through the front parlor and into the kitchen. Beneath an oak beam festooned with shiny pots and copper-bottomed pans, sat Ron and his brother, around a bar. Ron slid out from a stool, poured coffee in a mug and passed it over to me.

Sam stood, stuck out his hand, and grabbed my right hand.

"I don't want to seem unsocial," I smiled, "but I hope you aren't allergic to poison ivy, Sam."

He furrowed his brow, glanced down at my red hand, and kept his same firm grip. "Never have been in the past. It seems the least of my worries now."

"Does she know you're here?"

"No. I got in around 4. Ron let me in and I've been catnapping in the chair. I haven't slept well in a few days. I find it hard to relax when Sarah's in such a state of mind. I keep thinking she might do something harmful to herself… or me."

"Has she ever been violent?"

"No, but this time is different. She seems so comfortable with her religion that it is unnerving. It's hard to describe but it fits her right. It's like my wife has been taken over by a holy spirit who is showing her new things. She is the happiest she's been in years. Joyful in a child-like way. Part of me feels bad for wanting to bring the old Sarah back. But I'm at my wits end. We can't go on with her acting like this. I'm hoping she can get back on her meds and get back to being my Sarah again."

The pain was clear in his low voice. Sam was hurting, probably more than Sarah, because he was planning on a course of action that was going to hurt her, one way or another.

"I've heard good things about the psych center. They have a geriatric unit. That way she won't be in with the general population."

"You mean to say with the other, younger nuts?" Ron said.

I didn't reply. Just nodded my head and looked at Sam.

"Sometimes life sucks," was all he said.

As if on cue, Janey came around the corner.

"I'm going upstairs to wake her up and have her come down for breakfast."

We held our cups of coffee, listened to her footfalls going up the stairs, heard the creak of a door and a spatter of voices. Within a few minutes, Janey came back into the kitchen. Behind her was a plump woman, dressed in a white gown, barefoot, with her short hair frizzing out wildly from her oval head. Her smile was beatific, displaying shining white teeth that seemed to take up half of her face. Her nose was pugged and her eyes were bright blue.

When she saw her husband sitting on the stool, her expression remained the same. In a voice filled with genuine awe, she stated, "What are you doing here, Sam?"

Sam stood up and walked slowly over to her, giving her a hug and clasping her to his lanky frame. She sat down in a chair at the table and I moved over from the bar to be near her. I held out my hand and shook her rotund one.

"Hi, I'm Mitch Remmings. I'm a friend of Ron and Janey's. I'm also a Central County Police Officer."

"Oh, I'm so glad to meet you! I pray often for police

officers. Your job is so dangerous!"

"I'm here because I learned that you had been reported as missing. I want to help you get back on track so you can go back home with your husband."

She glanced over at Sam, appraisingly. "If he is my real husband. I've met three other men who look just like him."

Sam exhaled. He placed a hand on her thigh and squatted down on his haunches, looking up at her eyes.

"Honey, I don't know what's going on but you need help. I've made arrangements to have you examined at the hospital in Central City. They have a special unit for people with problems. Ron and I want to drive you there so you can talk to the doctors."

"Oh, I'll talk to them as long as they don't try to give me any medicine. When I take those pills, it's just like a shade is pulled down over my eyes. I can't see or think clearly. I can't even hear the Lord's voice."

"I'll make sure I tell them that, hon. Ron, will you go start up the car?"

Ron got up and left out the back door. Sarah turned to me and held out her hand, palm up.

"Officer Mitch, two nights ago, I placed my pills in my hands and prayed. I asked the Lord to show me if He wanted me to take those pills. The pills just flattened out and all that was left was just the empty capsules. I took that as a sign. I won't take any pills."

I've interviewed a lot of people. My whole job depends on me reading people and deciding if they are telling me the truth. Every instinct I possessed told me that Sarah, with her blue eyes wide and her voice dripping with a devout fervor, fully believed what she had just told me. Her earnestness was humbling. I flashed back to how every prophet in the Old Testament had been ridiculed by the unbelieving throngs when they revealed to them God's testimony.

"The doctors will help you, Sarah. They're good people."

"I know they are. But they won't understand. They won't listen."

She turned to me and her eyes bored into mine.

"Tell me, Officer Mitch, do you believe? Have you been born again? Are you saved?"

Without thinking, I reached out and took her hand.

"I believe, Sarah. I truly do."

She reached out and rubbed her other hand across the top of mine. She felt the roughness and looked down at my rash.

"Oh, my. You're hurt and needing the Lord's healing touch." Shutting her eyes, she prayed.

"Jesus, heal Mitch thy servant. Remove his pain and suffering and return him to good health. In your sweet name, Amen."

Janey stepped forward.

"Come on, Sarah. I'll take you upstairs and we can get your suitcase."

Sarah stood up, smoothed down her white gown, and passed by the piano in the parlor. She stopped, placed her hand on the keys, and played a short tune.

"I love to play the piano. The Lord can do so much. He uses music to soothe our souls. Do you think He can do miracles, Officer Mitch?"

"Yes, I believe He can."

"He can also allow His followers to use His power. He did it with Peter and John. He could do it through you, Officer Mitch."

"I don't know about that. I try to adhere to that old saying about not tempting the Lord thy God. He's needed to help other people, not an old cop like me."

Sarah froze, cocked her head, and said nothing. A few

seconds later, the wide smile returned and she stated," He's been with you in the past. He'll be with you yet again. Just believe."

She then followed Janey up the steps. I turned and Sam started up the stairs. "I'll keep an eye on her."

I placed my hand on the banister. I heard the slam of the back door and Ron walked into the kitchen.

"Are they ready?"

"Soon. They're just getting Sarah's things."

"Wow. She's worse than I imagined. Have you seen anyone else like this, Mitch?"

"She's delusional but non-violent. I think the problem will be when you guys get her to the psych center. She may balk about going inside. She definitely believes that she is hearing the Lord's voice."

"Yeah. It's unnerving but yet, in a weird way, inspiring."

I nodded my head. The line between sanity and insanity is thin and I felt Sarah was playing on both sides.

Suddenly, I heard the sound of breaking glass and a high pitched scream. I bolted up the steps onto the hall landing. Sam and Janey were tangled in a pile upon the hallway floor, both flailing to get up on their feet. The door to the attic was wide open. I ran up those steps and saw the smashed window. Shoving aside the boxes of clothes and Christmas decorations, I looked out the window. Sarah was straddling the peak of the shingled roof. She had her arms out front like a sleepwalker, stepping towards the end of the roof.

"Sarah!" I yelled, clambering through the shards of glass and the remnants of the broken window frame. "Stop!"

She turned her head over her left shoulder, beamed that same rapturous smile at me, and continued walking.

"Don't worry about me, Officer Mitch. The Lord protects those who love him even if they have only the belief of a mustard seed. He's calling me now. He'll watch over me. I am

His. I love you, Jesus!"

And with those words, she plummeted over the roof's edge.

The fall broke her neck and shoved several rib bones through her internal organs. The EMTs were there in six minutes but she had been killed immediately. Sgt. Bill Tiomminons came down and handled the death investigation. Coroner Randy Clinger picked up the body and made arrangements to have it taken back for viewing in Ohio. I gave Bill my statement, comforted Janey, Ron and Sam, and left.

I called off sick the next day from work. I also never went out and attended the burial, even though I should have.

I keep thinking that I overlooked something, some clue that should have tipped me off as to what Sarah was intending to do. I had been called to help out a poor woman and I had failed.

Whether or not she was delusional, there was no doubt in my mind. She thought she could walk on air and the cold pull of gravity triumphed over her belief. Yet, I still see the look of peace and glory in those wide blue eyes and the total lack of fear. In her mind, she was just following the words of her Lord.

And I could file this whole incident away as what happens when mental patients go off their meds, or as schizophrenics attempting to deal with their version of reality, if it wasn't for the cold hard fact that my poison ivy rash vanished. No more itching, no more scratching, no more scarlet bumps on my hand or wrist. Vanished right after a delusional woman touched my hand and said a prayer of healing. Yeah, you tell me that she was crazy. Just like Isaiah, Jonah, Jeremiah, Daniel and, now, added to that list, Sarah.

"Nothing will get you," Ruth said. "I promise."

The Night-Light

By Jeffrey Vavra

"I hope the new lamp I found at the salvage store," Ruth called out from the kitchen where she was putting away the dishes, "will make it easier for Jeremy to get to sleep. It's got a cute black bear holding an umbrella that—"

"Easier?" Corman angrily dropped his arms to his lap and mangled the newspaper he was reading. "You didn't leave it on when you put him to bed did you?" He had just finished a long stressful day in a series of long stressful days kowtowing to the demands--no, make that whims--of upper management. He was angry with himself for being afraid and not having the courage to tell them all to go to hell.

"I just thought—"

"Ruth, I told you that night-light business was over. Jeremy is seven years old now." Corman launched himself from the chair and headed for Jeremy's bedroom.

"Cory, please, Jeremy may finally be asleep."

The light from Jeremy's room escaped out from under the door and sliced into the darkness at the end of the hallway. Corman pushed the door open.

"What's that, who's there?" Jeremy said, sitting up.

"It's all right, Jeremy." Ruth rushed to his bedside ahead of Corman.

"I don't expect to see you sleeping with a light on again.

Do I make myself clear?" Corman picked up the lamp. He would have smashed it to the floor had Ruth not intervened and pulled it from his hand.

"But, Dad," said Jeremy, "I'm afraid."

"Afraid of the dark? You play outside in the dark until we have to drag you inside."

"Cory," Ruth said, "you're not making things better."

"All right, you handle this. I'm going to bed. I don't want any lights left on. Do you both understand?" Corman stared hard at both Jeremy and Ruth.

Ruth watched Corman leave. She then put the lamp out of the way on the floor next to the nightstand and gave Jeremy a hug.

"You're not going to turn the light out are you?" Jeremy asked. "Something will get me."

"Nothing will get you," Ruth said. "I promise." She gave him another hug and on her way out turned off the light.

Two hours passed.

Ruth, who had been reading in bed, heard Jeremy cry out and the dog bark.

"Cory, did you hear that?"

"Huh, what?" he asked, waking up.

"It's Jeremy!" Ruth dashed out the door and down the hallway into Jeremy's room, where she flipped on the light.

Jeremy reached out from the bed where he was on his knees, tears ran down his cheeks.

"Something was here! I could feel it climbing up the sheets." The words tumbled out from his trembling lips.

Ruth glanced from the bed to the floor and saw nothing. "It was just a bad dream."

"No, it wasn't a—"

"Yes, it was," Corman said, as he stepped into the room.

"I wasn't dreaming," Jeremy said. "Something was

pulling at the sheets here." He indicated a spot at the side of the bed.

Ruth, by reflex, pulled the sheets up to show Jeremy there was nothing wrong, and found her fingers slipped through slashes in the material.

"Oh, my," she said.

"See, I told you," Jeremy said.

"Let me see that," Corman said. "Your dog did this. He ripped it with either his teeth or paws. No boogeyman climbed onto your bed."

"Jasper, Jasper, where are you?" Corman called out.

Some small yips and the sound of a tail thumping the floor came from the opposite side of the room where the black lab lie.

"Look at him. He's cowering under the table. He knows he did something wrong." Corman walked over to the dog, grabbed it by the collar, and dragged it out from under the table.

"Jasper tore the sheets. Incident closed. Now go to bed. Both of you."

"It wasn't Jasper, Dad," Jeremy pleaded.

"Come on, Ruth," Corman said, impatiently. "Let's get back to bed. I have to be in early to work tomorrow."

"No! Please don't go." Jeremy began to cry again. "Can I sleep with you?"

"Ruth, don't coddle him!" Corman left the room, dragging the dog to the kitchen; its nails scratched the floor in protest. He opened the back door and pushed the dog out.

Heading back to his bedroom he called out, "Ruth."

"I've got to go now, honey," Ruth whispered. "You'll be okay. The dog's outside."

"Ruth!"

Ruth snapped off the light and quickly retreated from the room before Jeremy could say a word.

The house settled.

Jeremy rolled into a ball and cried himself to sleep.

Corman dropped off as soon as his head hit the pillow and exhaustion pulled Ruth into unconsciousness.

It was well into the night when a slipping, slightly scratching sound escaped the quiet. A gentle tugging on the bed sheets began, then harder, as if supporting weight.

Feeling the covers pulled down to the side, Jeremy awakened. He could feel the mattress giving in against the weight of whatever was out there. He dipped his head below the covers, believing the cocoon he fashioned around himself could protect him.

He said loud enough to whatever was out there to hear: "Go away." He felt the mattress sink closer to him. "Please go away."

Jeremy screamed.

Ruth bolted awake. Another scream. This time cut short.

"Jeremy!" Ruth tried to get out of bed, but Corman held onto her.

"We will not spoil that child," he said. "Let him learn to face his fears on his own."

This time they both heard a throaty growling.

Ruth ripped herself free from Corman. With Jeremy's screams playing repeatedly in her mind, she raced down the hallway, burst through the doorway, slipped on the braided throw rug, and landed on her hands and knees at the side of the bed.

Tears in her eyes, she looked up and thought she saw a shadow moving near the nightstand. She looked to the bed and began sobbing and pounding the floor with her fists.

Corman entered, his eyes immediately drawn to the bright red patch on the bed.

"Oh, my God," he said in disbelief. Jeremy was dead. Corman quickly scanned the room. The shock was rapidly shutting down his capacity to comprehend what was happening and acting on instinct alone, he managed to pick up the sobbing

Ruth and exit the room, careful to close the door behind them. Corman half carried half dragged Ruth to the living room where his hands numbly dialed 9-1-1.

The police arrived shortly thereafter. Conducting a thorough search of the house and grounds and finding nothing, the detective asked Corman and Ruth to join him in Jeremy's bedroom.

"Have you any idea what happened to your son?" the detective began.

"I...no, he woke us up with his screaming. Then we heard some kind of animal noises."

"Do you own a dog? The coroner on his way out corroborates your part about an animal being involved."

"Yes, but I put him outside," he mechanically said, and stiffly pointed toward the back of the house.

"That's what I thought. All I found was that lab out back, and it was docile and clean."

A uniformed officer asked for a moment of the detective's time. Excusing himself, he stepped away leaving Corman and Ruth to stare at the blood-soaked sheets of Jeremy's bed. The dried, rust color contrasted harshly with the clean, crisp, white bed linen.

"Will you look at that?" the detective said after he rejoined them. He walked over to the bed and crouched down to get a better look at something on the floor.

"Cute sucker this bear-lamp. It's so life-like. It has fur and everything," the detective said, as he picked up the black bear holding an umbrella over its head as a shade, and turned it in his hands. "I'll bet my kid would like something like this."

Then something caught his eye. "Ain't that the strangest thing? All that splatter from the attack and just the bear itself is touched. The lampshade is clean."

She was just lying there and when I rolled her over...blood
was all over her throat.

Prey

By Rex Munsee

    I downshifted my Ford F-150 into second gear as I began the long climb up the hillside to the Aerie, or so the wooden sign had informed me at the bottom of the driveway, as I turned off the dirt road. I had been here four years ago when Janey White had become the bride of Jamie Cippalla, a computer techie from California. It had been a summer wedding in late July; today was a muggy, dog day in mid-August. I wiped my forehead, running my AC along with having my windows rolled down, and drank the last swig of my IC Lite.

    The oaks and maples were beginning to lose their green vibrancy, changing into a stale emerald canopy as I broke out into a flat opening at the top of the foothill, which soon rolled into the Appalachians. Parked out front in the long swooping drive were a number of marked units, one orange and blue ambulance, and the SUV of Central County Coroner, Shaffer. I parked my truck, stepped outside into the heated air, tucked my shirttail inside the band of my khakis, adjusted my holster carrying my Glock .45, and set off down the blacktopped drive. At the front door, a uniformed county deputy looked me up and down before opening the door to let me in.

    "You must be Mitch Remmings?"

"Yeah. Detective Sam Davis called me. Is he around?"

"Yes. Sign in on the Crime Scene Entry Log. I'll escort you through the house."

House was the wrong word. Mansion was better. I followed the uniform through the front foyer with a sweeping cherry staircase leading to the upper level and through a sunroom with white furniture and teak colored chairs and desks, a sitting room with couches and leather recliners parked in front of a TV the size of my first house trailer, a sunken dining room with a table long enough to seat twelve, and a recessed bar that had more booze than any one gin joint in Central City. Then we crossed into a glass-ceilinged hot house leading onto a granite tiled deck. A kidney-shaped pool was to our left as we descended a flight of steps leading out to a groomed lawn.

I saw a group of men in sports jackets and loosened ties standing off to the side of a strip of flapping crime scene tape. Within the confines of the tape was a woman, face down, wearing a yellow bikini. Her blonde hair was streaked with blood and a small pool of blood had gushed out from beneath her throat. I spied a trail of blood leading back to an extended chaise lounge that had been tipped over on its side, probably by the woman as she jumped off of it. She had only run about 20 yards when she collapsed.

I stopped at the tape line and stared at the curved back and the side profile of the lovely face, partially covered by her hair. There was no doubt it was Janey. I thought of her parents, Jack and Sandy, of summer barbeques, winter toboggan rides, and girls' basketball games. As I stood lost in thought, Sammy walked alongside me.

"Mitch? Is that her? Janey?" he said softly.

"Yeah. Have her folks been told?"

"Not yet. 'Digger' Shaffer thought you might like to go with him to break the news."

"God, it's gonna kill them, Sammy. She was their only daughter."

"We still don't know all the details. Her husband, Jamie, got here around 3:00 pm. He called for her and got no answer. He called her cell and it just went to her voice mail. He walked out back and saw her lying here. He ran over to her and called us on his cell. He's inside now. The ambulance personnel treated him for shock and gave him a shot to calm him down."

I looked Sam in his grey eyes, noting the wrinkles and sweat that covered his face.

"What's the cause of death?"

"Massive trauma to the front of her throat."

"What kind of trauma? Blunt force, bullet wound, knife?"

"It looks like some kind of an animal ripped out her throat."

"That makes no sense!"

"I know but it's all I got now. The blood splatter guys from the PA State Police crime lab will be here soon. I'm just telling you what I've seen. It's too crude to be from a blade but something sliced or tore out her throat."

I glanced over at Janey, observed no other visible marks on her body, and again studied the crimson liquid leaked out onto the ground from her throat. Flies were already starting to buzz around her head.

"At least cover her up, Sammy. She was a good kid."

I walked over to Shaffer and shook his hand. He clapped me on the back and led me away from the throng of plain-clothes cops.

"Look, Mitch. I asked for you so you could stay with the Millers after we break the news to them. I know you guys are close."

"Okay. Let's go. I don't see much else I can do around here. Have you talked to Jamie yet about the arrangements?"

"No. Let's go inside and see what he can tell us. I'll at least find out what funeral home he wants me to take the body to after the autopsy."

I followed Shaffer inside, noticing how he was favoring his left hip as he walked. Age was settling into him, just as I felt it hit me hard when I saw a young girl half my age struck down. It ain't right to see someone who should be outliving you lying face forward in the grass.

Another uniform took us down a flight of steps into a spacious man-cave. Computers, stereos, TV screens, and X-boxes filled the room. In one corner was a glass curio cabinet, filled with old daggers and swords. Stretched out on a La-Z-Boy recliner with a washcloth upon his brow and a bottle of Petron on a glass-topped stand near his open hand was Jamie Cippalla. He reached up, removed the cloth, and pushed his elevated footstool down.

"Don't bother getting up. We won't be here long. I'm sorry for the loss of your wife, Mr. Cippalla. And I don't mean to be insensitive, but can you tell me what funeral home you would like your wife to be sent to when the police are done?"

"I'm not real familiar with places like that around here, as I'm originally from California. Wherever her parents would like her to be is alright with me."

As they continued talking, I sized him up. I had little to do with him after he married Janey. He had made a lot of money in computer games and programming, stuff that I truly didn't understand. I'd heard from Jack that their marriage had hit a rough patch but they were working through it. He was tall, around 6'6", thin, with whitish colored skin and contacts. I guessed him to be in his early thirties, although he seemed younger. Or perhaps, more immature. He wore a scraggly beard and mustache. I had an easy time picturing him staring into a computer screen in a dark room, alone, and vicariously living out his fantasy of living a life of adventure.

I stepped over to the curio cabinet, looking at the daggers, sheaths, and figurines of dragons and wizards. In several pewter frames were pictures of him, dressed in Renaissance-style clothing, holding a sword or a wand. None of the pictures included Janey, although there were other similarly garbed people standing with their arms clasping each other's shoulders.

As I walked back to Jamie and Digger, I heard the distinctive beep of a cell. Jamie grabbed it from out of his hip pocket, checked the number, and put the phone down on the stand by the Petron.

"In California, it's just noon. My boss usually calls me at that time. I'll call him back later."

"Can I have your cell number in case I have to get a hold of you, Jamie?" I asked.

"Sure." He rambled it off and I jotted it down on a folded paper I carried in my shirt pocket.

"Are you with the Coroner's Office, too?"

"You might say that. I'm a friend of Jack and Sandy's. I'll go over to their place with Mr. Shaffer to help break the news to them."

"Thank you. I'm too much of an emotional wreck to go over there now. Thanks, Mr. ...?" I hadn't expected him to remember me from one hurried introduction at his wedding over four years ago.

"Mitch Remmings. The cops told me you found Janey. You have my sympathy. She was a good girl. Her folks will take it hard."

He put his head down and just nodded, wiping his eyes with his balled fists.

"Yeah. It's so hard to believe. She was just lying there and when I rolled her over...blood was all over her throat. I freaked out. I don't understand it. We built this place so we would have privacy. Janey liked to tan herself in our backyard because no one was around to look at her."

"Why don't you sit back down, Jamie?" Digger said. "I'm sure the medicine the EMTs gave you will calm you down soon. We'll talk later."

As we wound down the driveway and pulled onto the dirt road leading us back to the macadam road that would take us in a few miles to Jack and Sandy's house, I leaned my head back into the leather seat of Shaffer's SUV that he used as a hearse. He pulled out a cooler from behind his seat and tossed me a bottle of water. I spun the top off and drank.

"What do you think did that to her throat, Bill?"

"I didn't get real close but I could tell that the lacerations were deep and jagged, almost a puncture type wound."

"How are you calling this one?"

"I think we can eliminate natural causes. Doesn't appear accidental. Nor suicide. That only leaves homicide."

"Could the cuts have been made by long fingernails?"

"Possible. However, I noticed Jamie's nails were chewed to the quick."

"I saw that, too. But I also know that when you truly cry, your nose fills up with snot. He had tears but no snot. I think he knows a bit more about Janey's death than he's pretending."

I was a Central County cop for 30 years. When I started out, I was always glad when the older corporal or sergeant would come out to the scene of a fatal car crash. They invariably delivered the death message to the next of kin. As time went by, I got older and that task drifted over to me. There is no good way to tell a father, mother or spouse that their son, daughter, husband or wife is dead. I'd learned to say it softly, give some detail, and find someone else to stay with the grievers as fast as possible. No one reacted the same – some went catatonic, some fainted, others collapsed into a fit of tears. Jack was in his garage, doors open, beer in hand, sitting on a lawn chair, listening to a Pirates game. I could tell by the panicked look on his face when he saw me step out of the passenger side and Digger from the driver's side that he knew Janey was dead.

Just then, the interior screen door banged open and Sandy walked into the garage. At first, her face was pleasant with surprise. She looked at her husband, looked again at us, glanced at the SUV in her drive, and sprinted over to Jack. She grabbed him by the shoulders. Jack stood up, held her, and waited. I broke the news. Sandy sobbed uncontrollably into Jack and he leaned against the front end of his Chevy, using its grill to keep him from falling.

The next few hours were a blur of grief, sadness, and activity. Jack and Sandy's brothers and sisters flocked to the house for support. I mostly stayed in the background until late evening. I did ask Jack if I could get a ride to pick up my truck at Janey's place. He told me the ride would do him good as he wanted to see Jamie anyway.

When we got there, all the lights were out except for the dusk to dawn lights. My truck was still parked where I'd left it. Jack went up to the door and rang the bell and knocked. No one answered. He came down the tiled steps, stopped, turned to look back at the house, and said in a low tone, "Where would he be?"

"That sedative they gave him could have knocked him out."

Jack turned and looked at me.

"Tell me straight up, Mitch. What are you thinking really happened?"

"I don't know. Yet."

"I know you do PI work. Consider yourself hired. I want to know what really happened."

I reached out and grabbed his shoulder. "I'll find out. Right now, just go back home and be with Sandy. One thing, I don't know much about Jamie. Can you give me some background on him?"

"Janey met him while she was in college. We don't have a lot in common. He plays a lot of computer games and spends his weekends role-playing knights and kings, or some shit like that. He made tons of money and Janey seemed happy. Though she had told Sandy that in the last year or so, they were spending more time apart. He didn't beat her and he wasn't into drugs. I tried to be supportive and kept quiet. All marriages function differently and theirs seemed to be working."

"Mitch, my little girl is gone. Dead. I don't know if I can get through this…"

I hugged him and led him to his car. He sobbed loudly. He stuck the key in the ignition and slowly backed out. I stood there, watching his taillights go down the long driveway. The night sky was speckled with stars. The mansion easily sat upon five acres of manicured lawn. It looked peaceful and quiet. The night had cooled things down and the humidity had slackened. There seemed no way that a stranger could have walked onto this property, found Janey lying in that lounger, sliced her throat and watched her stumble away to bleed out. Too much still made no sense. I decided to stop in and see Sammy at the station as soon as I could tomorrow.

I dropped a bag of doughnuts onto Sammy's desk, pulled out a nearby chair, and swiveled over to him. He raised his face up from the green glare of his computer, hit the "Save" button, rubbed his eyes and asked if I wanted some coffee. As he poured two Styrofoam cups full of black coffee from an ancient Mr. Coffee Machine, I opened the bag and took out a glazed doughnut.

"What kind did you get?" he asked, setting down my cup.

"The usual – glazed or plain."

"Good God! There must be twenty different varieties down at the Joe and Dough Shoppe and you always get the same kind."

"And your point is…?" I said, breaking the doughnut in half and dunking it in my cup.

"That you need to change. You're stuck in a rut."

"Just for that, my next doughnut will be a plain one."

After a few minutes of shop and cop talk, I wiped my hands on my pants and grabbed a plain doughnut. "Okay, tell me what you found out about Janey Cippalla's death?"

He flipped open his brown notebook, put his glasses on, and began to read.

"The autopsy was done down in Pittsburgh. Her throat had been lacerated by eight puncture marks. The punctures pierced her throat and then lifted upward, ripping her skin and jugular artery apart. She died from severe blood loss and trauma to the throat."

"Stop right there. Are you telling me she was attacked by a bird?"

"Traces of skin were left in the wounds. They were tested and are consistent with the hard yellow skin that makes up talons. What kind of a bird of prey we don't know."

"You're saying that a hungry eagle just flew past and decided to attack a 120lb woman who was sunbathing in her own backyard? That makes no damn sense!"

"Mitch! Do you want to hear what I've got or do you just want to bitch?"

I shut my mouth and nodded.

"No other signs of trauma were found. All internal organs were unremarkable."

Sammy put down his notebook, removed a sheaf of 8x10 photos, and tossed them my way. I skimmed through them, pausing to study the shots of Janey's throat. She had died an ugly and painful death.

Sammy pulled out a written statement from Jamie Cippalla. I read it, noting that it was detailed, and with no gaps or undocumented time lapses. It was roughly the same story that he had told Sammy yesterday concerning finding his wife.

"I take it that you've verified the cell calls and his errands in town?"

"Yep, the times match his cell and Janey's cell. Nothing odd about them. We found footage of him at the bank, the sub shop, and the library. During the time that Janey was killed, he wasn't at home. He was in town."

"Do you believe him?"

"Yes. I have to. He wasn't there when she died."

"Then, do you think he hired someone to do this for him?"

"I don't think you can hire a falcon or an eagle to kill someone."

"Are you thinking this was an accident?"

"I didn't at first. But Shaffer has backed off from a homicide ruling since I told him about this autopsy report. He's just listed it as a suspicious death."

"Sammy, you and I have both lived in this county our whole lives. I could buy a bear mauling, a buck impaling, or even a rabid raccoon bite, but I've never heard of a hawk killing anyone, let alone a woman sunning herself in a lounger. Have you?"

"No. But give me another explanation?"

"I can't but I'm working at it. My gut tells me this is a homicide. If Jamie Cippalla was smart enough to avoid doing

it, then he hired someone to do it for him. That's who I'm
gonna start looking for."

Investigations have changed since the advent of the
social network revolution. As much as I distrust computers, you
can't overlook the Web when you start checking out people.
So I went home and Googled Jamie Cippalla. I found his
Facebook page and clicked onto it. I delved into the company
he works for in California. I verified from Sam his criminal
history through NCIC. I also had memorized the license plate
displayed on his Prius parked at his house and ran that through
the Commonwealth JNET system.

Cippalla had no prior arrests. His Prius was leased. His
company was legit. And his Facebook page appeared to be
normal if you were into role-playing and Renaissance Fairs.
He had many pictures of himself with Janey. But once again,
no picture of them together when he was playing Frodo in
the woods. I clicked onto some links and found a group that
sponsored the Renaissance weekends. From what I could
gather, most of their rendezvous were held in an old reclaimed
coal strip job site down in the southern part of Central County.
The president of the club, William Johnson aka Greybeard,
lived in a small village where the Central River flows into
the Allegheny River, named Fordburg. I thought Mr. Johnson
should be my first interview. I Googled him and found his
address: 589 Wizard Ln, Fordburg Pa.

After doing my morning chores of scooping ground
corn into troughs for my horses and beef cows and wiping the
two horses down with fly spray, I showered, put on a short-
sleeved button-down shirt over a blue undershirt, twill work
pants, and Velcro sneakers. I left the shirt unbuttoned and
untucked so it would cover up my holstered .45 on my right
hip.

Twenty years ago when they eliminated the old Rural Route deliveries and assigned all Central County residents 911 addresses, it was determined that if you lived off of any public roadway on any length of a lane, you could name that lane anything you wished. So of course, people went into a naming frenzy. I was sure that was how Wizard Lane had been created. I'd patrolled this county for 30 years. I knew the Fordburg area but not exactly where Wizard Lane was. My guess was it was close to the location of the Renaissance Fair site. Forty minutes later, I was near a gated driveway with a sign proclaiming in Olde English that this was "Faire Country." Across the dirt roadway was another driveway with a small, log cabin just visible among some pine trees. The mailbox out front had stylized letters stating "Johnson - 589 Wizard Ln." My years of police experience led me to conclude that I was staring point-blank at a major clue.

I pulled my truck into the drive and parked near a well-kept cabin, with a huge variety of flowers in bloom along the front side. I knocked on the solid wood door, noting that the blinds were closed on the picture window. I heard a man's voice yell out and I stepped back from the door. I heard the shutting of an inside door and a dog's bark. Then the door opened and a man with an immense grey beard peered out at me.

"Mr. Johnson?"

"Who wants to know?" he said gruffly.

"My name's Mitch Remmings. I was told by a buddy of mine to get a hold of you about renting out a booth for the next Renaissance Fair?"

"You're just in time. We have our Labor Day Rendezvous almost filled up. What are you going to be selling?"

"I do carvings. I whittle whistles and scroll-saw cut wooden plaques."

"Then we have room for you. Let me get you the paperwork. Come on in."

He searched through a stack of paper piled on top of a massive oak desk. I glanced around at the pictures on his walls. Family. Harley Davidson motorcycle. Medieval Re-enactors. A hawk clutching a leather-wrapped forearm.

"I found it." He looked up and saw me staring at the pictures.

"Are these people from the Fair?" I asked.

"Yep. A fine group of folk."

"I bet. Must be one of them is into falconry?"

"Yeah. That's a picture of my son's hawk, Redtail. He can make that bird do anything."

"Really? Will he be at the Fair?

"You bet. He never misses them."

Johnson handed me the contract. I glanced at it. "Do you need a down payment?"

"Yep, that way I can guarantee you a spot."

I gave him a fifty dollar bill and he scribbled out a receipt. "When can I set up?"

"It opens at 4 on the Friday before Labor Day. Vendors can start setting up at 9."

"Okay. Thanks."

"By the way, who are you buddies with from the club?"

"Jamie Cippalla. I've known him for a few years."

"Christ, Jamie's been here a lot. He's good friends with Rick, my son."

"Maybe I'll get to meet him in a few weeks?"

"You bet. If you have any more questions, give me a call. My number's on the contract."

When I got back home, there was a message on my phone from Jack. In a strained voice he told me that the visitation for Janey would only be tonight from 6-8. The funeral would be at 11 tomorrow at the Rissinger Funeral Home with the interment at the Crestwood Cemetery.

I looked at the clock on my wall. It was 12:50. I went to the freezer and took out a patty of my own farm-raised hamburger. I picked some lettuce and a green tomato from the garden. I rolled out the grill, lit the propane tank and adjusted the flame. I tossed on the hamburger patty. As it slowly began sizzling, I sliced the tomato and an onion. I laid them next to the hamburger and pulled a sesame seed bun from the bread box. I cracked open a can of IC Lite, took a swallow, and poured some on the burger. I flipped it with a plastic spatula. I sat down in a lawn chair, drinking the beer and running Janey's death over in my head.

I decided not to pursue anything else until after the funeral. I didn't want to cause any kind of a scene at the viewing or the burying. It was going to be hard on the family as it was. I'd pick another day and time to put some pressure on the newly minted widower. I'd just closely watch him tonight and tomorrow.

It was right after the funeral meal that Jamie Cippalla approached me. We were in the basement of the Presbyterian Church, next to the cemetery. The previous night's viewing and this morning's funeral had gone along smoothly, accompanied by much sobbing and hugging. Jamie appeared dazed but he greeted the mourners by the foot of the casket with handshakes and hugs. Sandy White introduced him to the people who had arrived to show their respects. It was evident that Janey had been well-loved and Jamie was still unknown.

I was coming up the hallway from the Men's room when Jamie called my name. I looked to my right and he motioned for me to come into a small classroom. As I stepped in, he shut the door.

"Mitch, I've been doing some thinking. Janey was receiving some disturbing e-mails on our computer. She showed them to me and I just laughed them off. But, now that this has happened…. I think I should have taken them seriously. Can you come over to the house tomorrow night around 9? I'll show them to you."

"Sure, Jamie. What do you mean by "disturbing" exactly?"

"Descriptions of what she was wearing that day. Where she had parked her car in town. Stalker stuff."

I looked at him in alarm. "Why didn't you tell the cops about that?"

"I didn't even remember it until this morning while going through her e-mails. I thought with you being a retired cop, maybe I should have you look at them first."

"I'll be there at 9."

"Thanks, Mitch. I've already saved them to a secure file."

He opened the door, gave me the thumbs-up sign, and walked back down the hallway to the dining area.

The sun had slipped below the horizon and it was darkening into a hazy night as I turned into Jamie's driveway. I had the windows down and the AC off. It was still hot but most of the humidity had melted away. As I pulled into the circular drive around the front of the house, I noticed Jamie's Prius parked out front.

The outside lights were off. Two lights were shining from the windows on the side of the house. I knocked on the door. I heard no sounds of movement from within. I knocked again. Nothing but silence. I checked my watch. 9:01. I stepped back and that's when I spied a note taped by the doorbell button. I picked it up and looked. Shaking my head in dismay, I pulled out my glasses. Now I could make out the scribbled writing. "Mitch, come around back. Jamie."

I put the note in my hip pocket, placed my glasses back in my front shirt pocket and followed the tiled walkway around the side of the house. Green rhododendrons and honeysuckle bushes lined the wall. To my right was a hillock planted with roses, daisies, and gladiolus. I circled around the glassed-in sun porch and stepped onto the tile that surrounded the swimming pool. The submerged pool lights sparkled in the still water. I gazed out over the low brick wall to the back lawn where days ago Janey had died.

Towards the far side of the mowed yard, I could see movement. I hurried over to the wall and jumped down on the grass. The figure was walking towards the woods. I looked over my shoulder, saw no one on the back side of the house, and began crossing the open field. The figure had made it into the woods. I focused on the point where it had entered the trees. I was concentrating so hard on the mysterious figure, I failed to hear the slicing of wings in the still air.

It all happened at once. My head was buffeted by feathered wings and the back of my neck was gouged by talons. I threw up my hands to protect my face and collapsed onto the ground. I could feel chunks of flesh being ripped from my neck. I rolled over onto my back and punched out. I struck a bird's chest and saw the bird flutter up into the air. It hovered slightly and its head dipped forward and slashed my knuckles. Keeping it at bay with my left hand, I pulled out my Glock. I didn't have time to aim. I just pointed at the bird and pulled the trigger three times. Amidst an explosion of feathers, the bird dropped to the lawn.

I stood up, feeling the blood streaming down my back. The bird was a red-tailed hawk. I kept my gun pointed at it until I realized it was not breathing. I holstered my gun, stooped down and picked the hawk up by its talons. It had a wingspan of nearly 9 foot long and it was a mottled light tan in color. I guessed it weighed about 5 pounds. The talons were covered red from my own blood. Carrying the hawk in my left hand, I started walking towards the house.

I dropped the hawk on the tile floor next to the pool. I took off my shirt and bunched it against the back of my neck, which burned horribly. I took out my cell phone from my front cargo pant pocket, searching for Sammy's programmed number, with my vision dimming. I grabbed for my glasses, shoved them on my nose, and felt the swaying of everything about me. Loss of blood was affecting me quickly. I sat down in a metal deck chair, trying to make sense of the rolling list of phone numbers when I heard a low voice in the gathering darkness.

"I can't believe you killed that hawk."

I dropped the phone on a glass-topped table, pulled out my gun, and pointed it towards the voice.

"Why don't you come out, Jamie?"

A tall shadow stepped out from a recessed doorway. I leveled my gun at the form. Jamie took two long strides across the tiled floor towards me.

"Don't come any closer."

"Why, Mitch? I want to help you."

"Just like you helped Janey?"

He stopped. "What are you talking about? That hawk that attacked you? That's what killed her, too. I've already called 911."

"You're not stupid, Jamie. But you're a bad liar. You haven't called 911. You're just waiting for me to pass out. Then you'll kill me."

"That's not true. You're delirious. Let me help you into the house…"

He took another step.

"Stop! I'll kill you."

He froze and looked at me squarely. I could feel my strength draining as the blood kept gushing down my back. I had to get up and get to my truck. I hoisted myself from the chair, keeping the pool between him and myself. I slowly shuffled towards the gate leading to the side of the house.

"Mitch. Please. Just sit down. The ambulance will be here soon."

"How long have you and Rick been lovers?"

His face twisted from concern, puzzlement, surprise, and hardened into a scowl. His whole body stiffened and his mask dropped.

"I had no idea you were that good. I guess it is time to stop playing the game."

I turned to face him. I couldn't let him get too close or he would overpower me. I had to keep him at bay. But I was getting tired.

I heard the sound of running feet to my left. I swiveled towards the sound but too late. I was tackled and I hit the tiled floor. I only had time to shove the gun into the body and pull the trigger. The sound of the gun was muffled by his body. I felt the body tense and go limp. I shoved him off and rolled out from under. I kicked free and watched as his body slid into the pool.

"Rick!"

Jamie dove into the pool. I didn't stick around to watch. I managed to get to my feet and I stumbled down the steps. I slipped at the bottom and hit the grass. I pushed myself onto my hands and knees, took a deep breath, and realized that I had dropped my gun at the pool. I didn't have time to go retrieve it or the stamina. I had to make it to my truck. In the shape I was in, Jamie would kick my ass in seconds.

It was less than one hundred yards to where my Ford was parked. Each step felt like a thousand. My ears were ringing and I could feel my heart beating out of my head. I easily could have fainted. I just kept putting one foot in front of the other, expecting any minute for Jamie to clobber me from behind.

I was sweating in the warm August night but my body was shivering. I had also lost the shirt which was pressed against my neck and I could feel the blood sliding down my back and into the waistband of my pants. I began to stumble and reached out my hand. Instead of hitting the ground, it rested against the grill of my truck. I clung to the hood and took half-steps to the mirror, skidding my hand along the open window sill and onto the pull-up handle. My fingers refused to keep on the grip and the handle slipped out of my grasp. I grabbed it with my right hand and, double-handed, lifted up the release. I leaned into the door and rested against the inside of it, before grabbing the steering wheel. I pulled myself into the bucket seat, wiped my brow, shoved my left foot onto the clutch pedal, and twisted the ignition key. My truck started. I ground the gear shift lever into first, released the clutch and lurched forward. I swung through the lawn and made a lazy circle down the driveway. The air felt good as I forced my eyes open. I kept checking the rearview mirror and saw no signs of pursuit. I placed my foot on the brake and descended the winding driveway to the bottom. As I pulled out onto the road, I noticed the sign which read "Aerie."

"Not anymore," I said to no one but myself.

Within a mile, I pulled into the driveway of a mobile home and began hitting the horn. A fat woman smoking a cigarette came out and yelled, "What the fuck do you want?"

"Just call me a fucking doctor. Please." And with that, I placed my ripped neck against the headrest and passed out.

I woke up in a hospital. I saw the lights on a blinking

machine. I felt the tubes inserted in the top of my hand. I reached up with my free hand and touched the gauze and bandages around my neck. I shut my eyes again and slept.

When next I woke up, I was ravenous. I hit a button on a remote and my bed began lifting. I hit another button and the channel changed on the TV from "Days of Our Lives" to MSNBC. I punched a third button and an alarm rang. Presently, a stocky nurse came bustling in, dressed in multi-colored scrubs.

She grabbed my wrist and took my pulse. "How are you feeling, Mr. Remmings?"

"My neck is tender and sore."

"Yes. You are on some powerful painkillers. I'll call Dr. Mellano and tell him you're awake. Would you like some lunch?"

"Yeah. And would you give me a phone? I need to call some people."

Two days later, I was released. Sammy picked me up in my truck and drove me home. I walked gingerly across my yard, pushed open the door, and sat down at the kitchen table.

"Were you taking care of my animals?"

"You know better than that. I ain't no farmer, like you. The Swanson kid down the road has been tending to your livestock. For all I know, he's been drinking your beer, too."

"Speaking of beer, would you grab me one?"

Sammy opened the fridge door and lobbed me a can.

"Sure this won't clash with your pain medicine?"

"I don't really care. I'm thirsty." I cracked the can open and took a big drink. "So let me get this straight. I've been thinking on what you told me on our drive here. When you got to the house that night, you found Rick Johnson dead from my gunshot wound. Jamie had blown his head off with my gun and the dead hawk was still on the tile by the pool?"

"Right. If it had been around Christmas, I would have expected a partridge in a pear tree. The Homicide Report is just about done. I'll have it on the District Attorney's desk in a week. The ballistics all match. All the deceased were shot with your Glock. I'm sure the DA will rule this a justifiable homicide."

"Yeah, I'm not worried about that. You got the note from the door from my back pocket?"

"It was bloodstained but it was written by Jamie. Matched the tablet we found in his house."

"Good God, I was lucky. I should have known he was setting me up for an ambush with that killer bird of his boyfriend's."

"Now who would have ever thought of that? Rick Johnson had trained that bird of prey to attack humans? From what I've gathered on the Internet, that feat is nearly impossible."

"Well, my neck says otherwise. Have you talked to Jack and Sandy?"

"And Digger. He has made Janey's death a homicide. We've listed Jamie as the murderer and Rick as the co-conspirator. At least it's a clearance for murder."

"And it gives Jack and Sandy some peace of mind."

"True. From what I've gathered from Jamie's company, he had accepted a position back in California. He had fallen in love with Rick and he needed to get rid of Janey. Why he just didn't simply divorce her, I don't know."

"Probably didn't want to go through the notoriety of leaving his wife for another man. Plus, she would have gotten half their marital assets, plus alimony. Rick probably suggested the hawk plan while they were at the Renaissance Fair. It would have appealed to both of them. And, it made neither one of them the actual killer."

"What do you think tipped them off to you?"

"My own boneheadedness. When I met with Rick's father, he must have mentioned it to Rick. He put two and two together and came up with killing me. I'm sure Jamie was all for it."

I drank more beer. I opened the vertical striped bag and pulled out a bottle of prescription pain killers. I screwed off the top and swallowed an oblong pill. I washed it down with more beer.

"Did you deliver the death message to Bill Johnson?"

"Sure did. He took it hard. Asked a lot of questions. At first, he was angry at you. But when I told him about the gay lover bit with Jamie, he was even angrier at Jamie. So I couldn't get a good reading on Johnson."

"I think I'll just not show up at the next Fair."

"A wise choice."

He looked out the window and his cell beeped. He slid his thumb over it and read the text.

"Hey, I've gotta go. Lt. Winsott is short-handed and needs me to watch over the desk for a couple of hours. By the way, what's the prognosis on your neck?"

"Some plastic surgeon from Pittsburgh is going to take a look at it in a couple weeks when the stitches are out. As long as the muscles heal back up, I'll be happy. I could always grow a ponytail."

"Or wear turtlenecks."

"When will you turn back over my phone?"

"Why do you want it back? It's a flip phone and a TracFone. Spend some of your money and get a phone you can at least text on."

"I'll take that under advisement, along with your idea about wearing turtlenecks."

I walked out to the front porch and sat down on the cushioned porch swing. Sammy sped away in his unmarked

Taurus and I watched as the dust slowly swirled and dissipated in the muggy day. I knew he faced a pile of reports to complete. Homicide cases were always intense.

I decided to while the day away doing nothing. My neck hurt and I was hungry. I was also sad. Not for me but for Jack and Sandy. And even for Bill Johnson. Losing loved ones always hurt, regardless of the circumstances. I thought of Janey, killed by a man she loved. I thought of Rick and of the two things that he loved – Jamie and the hawk. In a way, I had murdered Rick and all that he loved. And I thought of the talons of that damned hawk piercing and clawing my skin. I wasn't sad for it because it was doing only what it instinctively knew how to do—be a predator. And I had been its prey, however briefly. I stopped swinging and walked into the kitchen. I had another Glock .45 in my gun safe. I felt it was time to strap it back on. Predators could come from any direction.

"I don't see it anywhere," she said anxiously.

You Never Know When In The Night *IT* Will Come

By Jeffrey Vavra

"Oh, there you are, Kendra." Merriam pulled the hostess aside. "We just got a phone call from our sitter. William's taken sick."

Completely untrue, but the lie couldn't hurt.

"Sick? I hope nothing serious."

"Just a touch of the flu," Merriam said, looking over to her husband David because she couldn't meet Kendra's eyes while telling the lie, "but he's uncomfortable and asking for us."

"Well you two run along," Kendra said, not trying to talk them into staying any longer. The sitter could certainly deal with a touch of the flu, she thought to herself. But she knew after the unexplained death of their first child, Ricky, two years ago they were rightfully overprotective.

"I thought you did it," the conversation began in the car.

"Me? Why me?" David asked. "What would make you think I did it? I thought you had it last."

"I know; I did. I forgot in the rush to get ready for Kendra's party. I was hoping…" she stopped.

"We could call and have the sitter do it," David suggested.

"That doesn't work and you know it," Merriam said. "We have to do it ourselves."

The truth was she didn't know it for sure. Like most superstitions, parts are grounded in fact. From the recesses of their brains, some dormant genes from an earlier evolutionary period warned them. It was something you saw your parents do and you believed their explanation of why they did it, so ingrained in our culture was the act. Like believing the Easter Bunny hides chicken eggs or a fat man dressed in a red suit comes down your chimney bringing presents.

"Let's just get home and finish the deal. It's nobody's fault," David said.

They were well into the evening hour.

You never know when in the night IT will come.

David drove fast, dangerously fast, rolling through stop signs, passing cars, cutting in and out of traffic.

While they lived only a few miles from the dinner party, the trip home seemed to take longer than the accustomed fifteen minutes.

David pulled into the driveway. The wheels squealed loud enough from the abrupt stop to announce their arrival.

Merriam hurried from the car, not waiting for David.

He caught up with her as she was turning the key in the lock.

They were greeted at the door by the sitter, Belinda. "I wasn't expecting you for another few hours," she said. "Is there something wrong?"

Entering quickly, they both put on phony smiles. "No, nothing wrong," Merriam said. "The dinner party was boring and David remembered he had some reports to complete before work tomorrow, so we decided to call it an early night."

David looked at Merriam. "Why don't you check on

William," he said. "I'll make sure Belinda gets paid."

"Yes, yes," Merriam said and quickly walked off. "Thank you for coming, Belinda," she tossed off over her shoulder.

"We will, of course, pay you for the entire time you were to be here," David said.

"That's very generous. Thank you," Belinda said.

David helped Belinda with her coat and held the door for her as she stepped out into the cool nighttime air.

Not taking the time, as usual, to make sure she made it safely into her car, David closed and locked the door, then ran down the hall where he saw Merriam coming from William's bedroom—her face unreadable.

"Is he—?" he asked.

"So far. Let's just find it and finish it. I left it on the dresser when I was getting ready tonight."

Both hurried down the hall toward their bedroom.

Entering first, David's eyes scanned the dresser's surface.

"Did you move it?" David said, not seeing it. He checked behind the picture frames holding photos of their visit to Disneyland two years ago when Ricky was still with them.

Merriam opened a small mahogany box where she kept her watch, assorted bracelets and necklaces thinking she may have put it in there and forgotten. "I don't see it anywhere," she said anxiously.

David collapsed to his knees and peered under the dresser. He hoped the shiny exterior would light up like a lighthouse beacon in a storm allowing him to hone in on its location.

Nothing.

His mind wandered a moment. He speculated about what was done with the piece and its value to "IT". He used the word "IT" refusing to assign a sex and humanize the intruder in any way.

Merriam opened the top drawer of the dresser thinking that maybe she had brushed it into the drawer when she pulled out socks for the party. She mercilessly pulled and pushed the bundles of socks back and forth praying she would see a pearl of white floating in the sea of dark-colored footwear. She saw nothing. Not knowing what else to do she ravaged the drawer again more in frustration than thoroughness.

She closed the drawer and with David's help pulled the dresser from the wall to check the floor.

Again nothing. Anywhere.

David was desperate. "Where else?" He saw the clock on the dresser flip to 11:58pm. "We're almost out of time.

"The kitchen, we were in the kitchen, too," Merriam said.

If the situation hadn't been so grave they might have both laughed at the act of the two of them trying to get through the bedroom door at the same time.

Oblivious to the hideous amount of noise their shoes created in the stillness on the dark stone tile floor, they raced down the hallway to the kitchen and barged through the swinging door. The door rebounded off the refrigerator with a heavy WHOOM sound.

Their eyes darted from counter to desk to table.

Merriam headed for the sink area, hoping she might yet find their treasure on the paper towel where she and William had once put it.

The area around the sink was empty–except for the paper towel.

Merriam looked up at David, panic in her eyes. "Belinda wouldn't have thrown it away, would she? We'll give it one of ours."

"We don't know that will work."

"We have to do something."

David again surveyed the counters hoping that from another angle the results would be different. There…was that it under the phone…on a tissue. "Got it."

Merriam followed his gaze and saw their "Holy Grail."

You never know when in the night IT will come.

David, with Merriam close behind, snatched the tissue and took off down the hallway toward William's room.

Pulling up outside his door, they both took a big breath then quickly moved through the door to the side of William's bed.

They stopped and looked down at their son. Not moving they watched him, listening, eyes focused on his figure. The blankets slowly rose and fell and they heard breath escape through his lips.

Relieved, David carefully pushed his hand beneath William's pillow and placed the small incisor there.

Glancing back over his shoulder at Merriam they exchanged relieved smiles. Both physiques noticeably relaxed, the vise around their chests loosened.

Everything was all right now. The tooth was in its proper place for the Tooth Fairy to complete the cycle.

In an age when superstitions fall by the wayside by the truckload, some are maintained in a convoluted and nearly obscured form without knowing it.

They had learned the hard way.

Ricky.

An archaic barter system, established before anyone paid attention to such things, a bribe is given.

In exchange, The Tooth Fairy had to leave something— your child's life.

You never know when in the night IT will come.

They control or are connected to every major company in the United States and, possibly, the world.

The 100

By Rex Munsee

Standing at my office window, 56 stories high, and viewing all the twinkling lights usually fascinates me. The Hudson River winds a dark ribbon below and the energy of the city reverberates upwards and I can feel its pulse thrum through me. However, tonight, with Christmas just two days away, it all struck me as gaudy obstacles. The holidays had brought forth a longing for home that was churning my stomach. I wanted to escape the concrete and noise and be back at my Mom and Dad's in State College. To aid in my homeward drive, I already had my car packed and parked in the underground lot. I was just catching up on some insurance paperwork and waiting for the outbound traffic to dwindle. I planned to hit the road around 10, drive out of the city, cross into Jersey, hit 80, and speed west as fast as my little Suzuki could into the rolling hills of PA.

My laptop beeped. I left my reverie and walked to my desk. Punching the key, the e-mail from my boss, Bill Trezco, opened up.

"Brad, I really need to talk to you. I'm in my office. Come on up. You know the codes. Trez"

I glanced at the screen, 8:02 pm. I could spare him a half hour. Maybe he had some good gossip to spill. Even though Bill was my boss, we had a good relationship. He was older than me, around 50, but we shared a love of American history and of chasing women. We also were both good at calculating risks, a talent we had put to good use in our jobs as arbiters of what companies we would accept as clients.

I put on my houndstooth suit jacket and tossed my overcoat across my left arm. I shut down the laptop, flipped off the light, and watched as the outside lights speckled the inside of the office. I still wanted to go home. As soon as Bill was done jawing with me, I was hitting the elevator all the way down.

I shut and locked my office door. I walked down the carpeted hallway to the far corner where the sets of elevators were parked. I jabbed the up arrow and heard the smooth hiss of the car coming my way. After a soft ping, the door opened. I was surprised that a janitor was inside, beginning to push his cart brimming with rags, cleaners, and vacuums, out onto my floor.

"Working late, buddy?" I asked casually as I stepped back.

"Yeah, I'm catching up so I can head home to Philly for Christmas."

He was an older man, easily seventy, mostly bald with a round belly straining against his shirt. Around his wattled neck hung a pair of half-lens reading glasses which he grabbed and perched on his nose as he looked up at me.

"I know what you mean. I'm from Pennsylvania too and I can't wait to get home."

"It's the best state in the union. Philly's been my home all my life. I've traveled a lot, England, France, but there's no place like home."

"Well, have a good Christmas. I have to see my boss and then I'm out of here."

"Take care, young man."

Minutes later, I was lowering myself into the leather chair in front of Bill's desk. Bill was in his side bathroom and I noticed the topper from a bottle of single malt whisky was lying next to the decanter. I heard the toilet flush, the water run in the hand sink, and the snap of the lock as Bill walked out.

He made a straight path to the decanter. His tie was draped around his neck and his grey-peppered hair was slicked back. Lines of perspiration flowed down his cheeks and large ovals of damp sweat circled under his armpits. Shakily, he poured the whisky into a glass tumbler and tossed it down his throat. He shuddered and then turned to me.

"Brad, I've done it this time. They're out to get me!"

His blue eyes were widened in fear. In the seven years that I had known him, I had never seen him like this.

"Bill, what the Hell is going on?"

He poured me a drink and brought it over. As I was holding it, he poured himself another and carried it over to his desk. He sat down heavily in his leather chair and swiveled it to look out the window, at the same view I had of the Hudson, only three floors higher.

"I have stumbled onto a conspiracy so big, that I can't get out of it. My just knowing about it ensures my death. I'm thinking whether I should just jump off the roof first or wait for one of them to kill me."

"Maybe you shouldn't sit in front of the window," I joked.

Quickly, he grabbed a remote and pressed a button. The curtains lowered, blocking out all light from the outside. He swiveled back to me, upended his tumbler, drained it, and set it back down.

"Brad, let me tell you what happened. Hold your questions until I finish. This is going to sound crazy and it should be crazy… but it's true!"

"Okay. I'll shut my mouth and listen."

"They call themselves the 100. I agree that's not terribly original. I don't know the names of all 100 but I do know the names of some of them. They are wealthy beyond our imaginations. They control or are connected to every major company in the United States and, possibly, the world. Our government has been under their direction for two centuries. Wall Street, railroads, mining, computers, and universities – their members either created or still exist in those structures."

"For you see, they are immortal. That's the only way I can describe it. Every one of them should have died centuries ago but they have found a way to delay death! With their skills and knowledge and with time on their side, they ride out all competition and wait for their enemies to die. Then, they purchase or take over whatever they desire. That is how they've managed to insinuate themselves into all commerce, government, and religions."

Bill lifted his glass again and shook the melting ice into his throat. The sweat was still sliding down his cheeks.

"I discovered this when I was on vacation last week. Remember when I decided to visit the Caribbean? I booked a berth on a small tourist liner and launched from the NYC harbor. My plan was to go to the island of Nevis and, perhaps, St Croix to do a little digging into the boyhood history of Alexander Hamilton. And, while on the way, do some drinking, gambling, and looking for lonely women. Well, there were no women my age on board- just a bunch of senior citizens who were also heading to the Caribbean. I was invited to play poker with them one night. Good God, if only I had begged off and went to my room to read!"

"There were three of us. George, a rugged, well-built man who was easily over 6'2"; Tom, a shorter, red-haired man who loved to talk; and Frank, a chubbier fellow with a quick wit and great sense of humor. Over cards and glasses of beer and rum, we partied the night into the redness of dawn. My three elder companions seemed damned wealthy and well-rounded. No topic drew a blank stare from them. They easily conversed about politics, military tactics, finance, and farming with a skill that was stunning. They quizzed me about the insurance industry with an insider's knowing talent."

"We ordered breakfast and I fell asleep awaiting its delivery. Before I drifted off, I heard them talking about their boyhood days in Virginia and of running their farms. When I awoke, my breakfast was cold upon a tray at my side, and my three companions had departed. I stumbled off to my berth and spent the rest of the day sleeping. In the evening, I found my companions in the dining area. They invited me to eat with them and I met their lady friends, who were all much younger than them, and who weren't introduced as their wives."

"Again, we ended up at a table in the warm night, drinking rum and playing poker. This is how I spent the four day trip to the island of Nevis. All of my companions stated they were going island hopping and their first stop would be St Martens. Upon arriving at that beautiful island, I shook their hands and hugged their female friends, as they all departed. Within hours, I was walking upon the gangplank onto Nevis. I missed my congenial older buddies but I was checking into my hotel and about to begin my hunt for the early days of Hamilton."

"As I slipped off my shorts and tossed them onto the floor, I heard a metallic clunk. As I'd removed my wallet and keys from the pockets, the sound startled me. I picked up the khakis and in my back pocket, I found a thumb drive. As my room had no access to a computer, I slid the drive into my suitcase and decided to look at it when I returned to New York."

"For the next four days, I found little left of Alexander

Hamilton's formative years. A couple of historical markers and a mention in the library of his mother, father, and brother but that was all. I did consider renting a boat to St Croix where he had spent his teenage years but I decided to just lie on the beach and soak up some sun."

"On the fifth day, I packed and was waiting at the lobby to embark on the liner to take me back to the city. I picked up a newspaper and read that a small motorboat had capsized in the Caribbean and all were feared dead. It stated they were three female tourists from the states. No pictures accompanied the article and no further details were printed. I briefly thought of the three ladies I'd traveled down from NYC with, but since no mention was made of George, Tom or Frank, I thought no more of it."

"Four days later, I was back home in my apartment. I'd arrived late and had slept in. It was Sunday and I was tossing my dirty clothes into a basket when I discovered the thumb drive. I shoved it into my laptop's port and the screen opened. To my surprise, it was a video message by one of the three lady companions, the auburn-haired girl who had been with Frank. Her face was tight with emotion and her voice was jagged with fear. She begged me to believe her and to take this message to the news media. She pleaded not to take it to the police or anyone in the government. She stated her name, address, and phone numbers. Then she said she would be dead within hours, probably in an event that would look like an accident!"

"She went on giving the same spiel that I just gave you about the 100 and what they were involved in. Her last sentences are what caused me to shiver in fear and start my mind to race. It sounds like science fiction or horror written by Zelazny or King but it's the truth. The three senior citizens who I had played cards with on the ship were George Washington, Thomas Jefferson, and Benjamin Franklin!"

"Get out of here! What the Hell were you smoking on

that ship? Bill, listen to what you are saying!"

He glared at me with a wild fury. He lowered his head and breathed deeply. When he lifted it, his eyes bore directly into mine with an earnestness and sadness that impaled my heart.

"Just hear me out. That was my first reaction until I logged on the computer and Googled Sarah Anne Willminton, of Newark NJ. The Newark Star-Ledger obituaries popped up first. On Dec 18th, Ms. Willminton had been presumed lost at sea in the Caribbean. With her had been two other female traveling companions. There was a photo with the obit. Sarah was the red-haired girl from my ship, the same one who had somehow managed to slip the thumb drive into my hip pocket. And now she's dead. It took me a little more time on the Internet but I found the news articles that were published about the accident. The other two girls, Brandy O'Leary and Michelle Brandt, their bodies had washed up on the shores of St Marten. From photos I've found on-line, they were the other two girls with my elder buddies from the ship."

I picked up my drink, felt the moisture on the outside of the glass, and slid my fingers up and down the cool sides. A blur of thoughts clouded my mind, all of them telling me to get Bill to someplace where he could regain his composure.

"Listen, Bill. Why don't you come with me to my folks' place in State College? You can celebrate Christmas with us. Unwind. Relax. Think things through. A few days in the wilds of PA will give you a new perspective on things. I'm already packed and I'm leaving right now. Come on."

I left my glass and stood up.

"Okay," Bill said, relieved. "At least at your parents' place, no one will find me. I'll have a safe place to stay and decide what to do. I've already hidden the thumb drive. I mailed it to a friend of mine yesterday."

"Believe me, it's the town-that-time-forgot. Nothing but

trees, deer, and cows."

"Alright. Let me gather up my stuff and shut down my computer and I'll be ready."

"Great. Hey, I've got to use the bathroom. Can I use yours?"

"Yeah. Go ahead."

I walked into his private bathroom, shut the door and turned the lock. I used the toilet, flushed it, and was washing my hands when I heard a muffled noise in the office. I grabbed the doorknob but it would not turn. I wrenched it back and forth, but the knob refused to turn. I heard a rustling of clothing and loud gasps of breath, followed by a gurgling and coughing.

"Bill! What's going on? Let me out!"

I stood back and kicked the door. After the fourth kick, it splintered in the middle by the knob. On the sixth kick, my foot busted through the door. I squatted and peered out the jagged hole. The lights had been turned out and with the curtains shut, I could see nothing. I kicked the knob again and this time, the knob fell to the floor on the other side. I shoved the door open. The light from the bathroom illuminated the office interior. A silhouette of a hanging man dangled from the ceiling fan above Bill's desk.

I ran to the door and turned on the lights. The hanged man was Bill. I jumped onto the desk and hoisted him upwards, trying to slacken the cord that was biting into his neck. With both arms lifting his weight, I could not untie the cord. I let go, pulled out my pocket knife, and sliced the electrical cord. Bill's body plummeted to the carpeted floor with a heavy thud. I scrambled down and loosened the cord around his neck. His face was purpled and vomit had bubbled out of his mouth.

I grabbed my cell and hit 911. I shouted directions and disconnected. I unloosened his shirt and began CPR. I never found a pulse but I continued giving the compressions and breaths until I heard a loud pounding at the door. I shouted and a crew of EMTs burst in. I collapsed back on my butt and was catching my breath, wiping my forehead, as they started hooking him up to a defibrillator. A woman dressed in a blue jumpsuit asked me some questions and I answered honestly.

Within a few minutes, they removed all their equipment. Two men wearing police uniforms came in, looked around, and interviewed me. Two other men wearing black jackets that said NYC Coroner's Office arrived with a gurney. After the two cops took some pictures, the NYCCO slid Bill into a black body bag, hefted him onto the gurney, and wheeled him out the door.

I had made my way back to the bar and was pouring some whisky in a glass when another man, wearing a black overcoat and hat, came walking in. He briefly talked to the two cops, who pointed at me, and then came my way, flipping open a notepad.

"Mr. Shaffer?"

I nodded.

"I'm Detective Mueller. I'll be handling your friend's suicide. First off, the two uniforms told me that Mr. Trezco was your boss and he had made some comments about killing himself. Is that true?"

"He said that but I didn't believe him. He was coming back to State College with me for the holidays."

"Yeah, the holidays are deadly for lonely people. From what I've gathered, he was divorced, no kids… just his job here."

"I think he has a younger brother somewhere in Jersey, he wasn't close to him."

"I'll make some calls. He might be the next of kin. One more thing- why do you think your boss locked you in the bathroom?"

"I don't know. I was on my way back to my office."

"Must be he thought you'd have stopped him. Here's

my card. You can cut out if you have somewhere else to go. I'll call you here at your work if I need anything else from you."

"Thanks. Please do call if I can help you in any way."

"Just hope that my next shifts are better than this one. It's not even Christmas and this is my third suicide."

I drained my drink, picked up my overcoat, and left. As I stepped onto the elevator, a strange thought flashed into my head. I hit the 56 button and stopped at my office floor. As I walked out, I stopped at the door labeled "JANITOR". I wasn't surprised when the door was unlocked. Inside was the cart. I grabbed the vacuum and lifted it. All that was left of the electrical cord was a short length attached to the base. The rest of it had been wrapped around Bill's throat.

I thought of finding Detective Mueller and telling him but Bill's warning about saying nothing to the police echoed through my mind. After what had just happened, I was placing great belief in everything Bill had said. I returned to the elevator, descended to the basement parking garage, made sure no old men were present and unlocked my car. I didn't quit looking into my rearview mirror until I was westbound on I-80.

I stayed at my Mom and Dad's for two weeks. I never went back to NYC for Bill's funeral. I felt bad about that but I was worried that someone may have been watching. During the middle of the night, I returned to my apartment and took some belongings. As I somewhat suspected, there was a manila envelope waiting for me at my box. I recognized Bill's printing and the outline of a thumb drive. I stuffed it, unopened, into my briefcase and left.

Since that night, I've never been back to NYC. I resigned from my job and broke my apartment lease. I work as a bartender now, out on the West Coast. I move around a lot and I look over my shoulder frequently. I have the thumb drive in the hands of an attorney who knows where to mail it if I don't contact him at 9:00 on the first of every month. I'm hoping that will be enough to deter the 100 from murdering me because, when it comes down to it, I'm not a spy or hero. I can't fight them and win. If I leave them alone, I'm hoping they'll just forget about me.

After all, wasn't it Ben Franklin who said, "God helps them that help themselves?" And we all know what a killer old Frank was.

My headlights showed upon a girl standing alongside the berm, next to the passenger side of her car.

The Stranger On Route 8

By Rex Munsee

Lightning flashed in the midnight sky. The scent of rain was in the air and the humidity was stifling. I had my left arm crooked out of my open driver's side window and was inhaling deeply on my Camel cigarette. The oncoming storm was knocking the radio station on and off and I reached down and spun the knob to kill it. The silence was punctuated by the low growl of thunder and the whining of the engine in my Ford pickup.

I had clocked out at midnight at the glass plant. I was speeding down Route 8, heading towards Union City, looking forward to seeing my girl, Mary. I was hoping to get there before the storm hit full on. She had told me on the phone before my shift started that she really wanted to see me and she'd be waiting up for me. I knew what that meant. She'd have a cold beer and hot kisses ready for me. I had Sunday off and I could spend all tonight and tomorrow with her. God, I loved that girl. She was the best thing that had happened to me in years.

Once I got out of the rat race of Erie traffic, the pavement opened up to the sparse farmlands in Greene Township. Here and there were small houses and old farms, with a few lights still on in their rooms. In rural Erie County, most folks were already asleep. The ones that weren't were either hitting the pool halls in Erie or entangled in their woman's arms. A position that I so wanted to be in that I hit the gas pedal and watched the needle climb over 80. The breeze felt good on my tired eyeballs. The inside of the hot end at the glass plant was like a liquid hell and even through my safety goggles, I could feel the fire from the blast furnace as it reduced the sand into molten glass. But all of that was blowing away like the leaves loosened by the storm winds which flurried in front of my headlights. I was thinking of Mary. Of her smile. Of the sight of her boobs as she shrugged out of her bra. Of the sound of her nightgown whispering down her skin to the floor.

I was in fifth gear and the needle was pointing to 90mph.

Rain had started to pelt my windshield. I turned the wipers on, rolled my window up to halfway, and flicked out my Camel. Off to my right, I could see the taillights of a car. They didn't look right; they weren't in the southbound lane, but over across the ditch. I took my foot off the pedal and hit my brake. My headlights showed upon a girl standing alongside the berm, next to the passenger side of her car. I hit my clutch with my left foot and braked with my right. I pulled off in front of her car.

I put the gear shift lever on the column to neutral and jammed on my emergency brake. I opened my door and kept my truck engine idling. I walked over to the girl. She was young, with coal-black hair. Her skin was pale; corpse-like. She had a silver bar pierced through the corner of her mouth. Barely covered by a halter top were several tattoos, one of a dragon and one of a unicorn. Her shorts were ripped and cheap sandals were all that separated her feet from the wet blacktop. All this I saw amidst jagged explosions of overhead lightning.

"What's wrong with your car?" I asked.

"I don't know. It just shut off."

"Didja run out of gas?"

"No, I filled it up in town today. I tried calling my Dad on my cel but I can't get through."

"Probably 'cause of the storm. Look, I'm on my way to Union City. This storm is about to hit hard. Standing alongside the road ain't a good idea. I can drop you off in town or if your folks' place is on the way, I'll let you off there."

She looked up at the storm, looked at her car, and looked at me. I could tell she was scared but there seemed something else in her eyes – a deep sadness. Perhaps even a loss.

"I don't even know you."

"Look, my name's Luke Hammond. I live outside of Union City on a farm. I work at the glass plant in Erie and I've been stuck on the graveyard shift there for the last five years since I graduated high school. And I'm in a hurry to get to my girlfriend Mary's place and you ain't gettin' me there any quicker. You can stay here in the dark in the storm or you can ride four or five miles into town and call from a payphone. It's your choice. I won't force you."

She chewed her lip and shook her tousled head. The rain was hitting harder. "Just let me get my purse from my car."

I trotted back to my pickup and jumped in. I reached over and pulled up the handle and swung open the passenger side door. The wind jerked it out of my hand and rain blew inside the cab. The girl jumped in and shut the door hard. She was wet and shivering. She hunched near to her door, like a dog expecting a kicking, and I noticed she had one hand on the handle.

Since the engine was still running, I released the emergency brake, slid out the clutch and steered back onto the southbound lane of Route 8. I pulled the knob out on the headlights and put the wipers on fast.

"What's your name?"

"Sherry Winston. I live off of Jennings Lane just past the convenience store before you get to downtown Union City."

"Ok. Do you want me to drop you off there or at the gas station?"

"Just drop me off at Jennings Lane. I'll walk home. It's not far.

"Even in this rain?"

"Yes, I've been wet before. It feels good…sometimes."

I glanced over at her and saw she was now clutching her purse. And I could smell a scent that reminded me of when we opened up the silo doors on the farm – the pungent odor of decomposition. I didn't know what she meant about feeling good when she got wet but I didn't ask her to explain. A small part of my brain was telling me that picking her up was not a good idea.

"Winston. Let's see… are you any relation to Merle Winston? I went to school with him."

"He's my Dad's uncle. My dad is Bob Winston. Do you know him, Mr. Hammond?"

I ran that name through my mind. I didn't know him but I had heard about him. Something about his sister? And a drowning in Lake Erie.

I looked straight ahead into the growing storm. "Not really."

Silence. When I glanced back over, she was pulling her fingers through her wet hair. And the smell of decay was growing. I saw a road sign stating "Union City, 3 Miles". It was going to be a long three miles.

"Hey, where were you coming from before your car broke down?"

It was her turn to look out the side window at the storm. She mumbled "Lake Erie. I was helping my boyfriend on his boat. We caught some fish and we cleaned them. I think that's why I smell kind of fishy. And…"

I glanced at her, saw a tear sliding down her cheek.

"Go on, Sherry."

"It was a bad day. That's all. Really bad. We broke up."

I just nodded my head. I grabbed a pack of Camels from my T-shirt, shook one out, stuck it in my mouth and pressed in my cigarette lighter. The rain was fierce but steady. I had to slow down to 50. When the lighter popped out, I lit the end of my Camel. I exhaled blue smoke and she looked at me in a disapproving manner.

"You don't smoke?"

"No. Bad for your health. Not that it matters sometimes. Things die, regardless of what you do to save them."

This hundred-pound girl was making me uncomfortable. Her paleness, ebony hair, soft voice—all I could think of was how much she looked like a wet corpse. I blew out more smoke, which masked the smell of decay inside the cab.

Through the downpour outside my windshield, I could see the lights of the gas station.

"Are you sure you don't want to be dropped off here?"

"No, my road is just beyond that."

I slowed down to 35 as I entered into the outskirts of Union City. I looked to my right and my headlights reflected upon a road sign.

"Pull over here! That's my road." Gladly I spiked my brakes and steered my Ford alongside the berm. She flung open her door and jumped out. She turned, tossing a gutted trout wrapped loosely in a paper towel from her purse onto my seat. "Here, I caught this today. I was taking it home to my Dad. I don't have any money. Thanks for the ride."

"Be careful!" I shouted as she slammed the door. She

walked into the darkness and I lost sight of her in the pounding rain. I inhaled on my Camel. Cranked down my window to let some fresh air inside to push out the smell of rot. I rubbed my chin, blinked my eyes, and pulled back out onto Route 8.

I made it through town and started picking up speed. Thoughts of the odd girl were receding, replaced with happy thoughts of Mary. Just two more miles. I tromped onto the gas pedal. The rain was sluicing off my windshield. The road was covered with water and it was lying heavy on the blacktop. I steered into the curve and I could feel the back end of my pickup fishtail. The rear end slid across the center-line. I counter steered but it did no good. My truck spun wildly. I hit the brakes and watched frantically as I flew off the roadside. Through the rain, I could see the tree trunk. I felt the shock of impact as the steering wheel jammed into my chest. My head speared the windshield.

"MARY!"

Sherry Winston knocked on the door of her granddad's house. The sun was out, drying out the yard from last night's storm. She had slept fitfully until 10. She had showered, changing into blue jeans and a flannel shirt. As she walked over to her granddad's house next door to her own, her brain was abuzz with questions as she approached his front porch.

The door swung open.

"Well, good morning, Sherry! What brings you out so early?"

She stepped through the doorway, pecked her granddad on his cheek, and stepped back.

"Morning, Grampa. I need a cup of coffee, a ride to my car, and to ask you some questions. Can you help me out?"

"Certainly. The coffee pot is already on. You still take it with cream and sugar?"

"You know I drink it just like you like it. You taught

me how."

Bill Winston chuckled, rubbed his hand over his bald head, and led his granddaughter into the kitchen. He poured both of them a steaming cup, shoved over the cream and sugar, and listened as she told her story about her strange ride. She explained about her car shutting down along the roadside, how a young man driving an old pickup truck with a gear shift lever on the steering wheel had stopped, talking about coming home from a graveyard shift from the glass plant, hurrying to see his girlfriend and about how fast he drove. He smoked Camel cigarettes from a pack that he'd had rolled up in his T-shirt sleeve and he wanted her to use a payphone at the gas station. And how, even though he did nothing wrong, she instinctively was afraid of him.

Bill Winston stopped drinking his coffee. When Sherry was done talking, he looked her in the eye.

"You're telling me the truth? You haven't been looking up old stories from the Internet have you?"

She crinkled her face. "No. I don't even know of a Luke Hammond. Why?"

"Back in 69 or 70, Christ, I can't even recall exactly when… but I know it was after your Aunt Sherry, your namesake, drowned in Lake Erie."

Bill Winston paused, letting the memory of his oldest daughter cascade over him until he again found his voice. In a low tone, he continued. "Sorry, Sherry. It still hurts." He swallowed a sip of coffee. "Let's see, it's pushing 50 years ago, easy. The glass plant in Erie closed down in 80, that I remember because your Dad lost his job when it did."

"Anyway, Luke Hammond was coming home on Route 8 late at night. He was going too fast and lost control of his pickup out on that sharp curve the other side of Union City. He was killed instantly. So sad. He was a good kid. It was big news back then."

"In the years since, I've heard a couple of stories from people after they've been hitting the bottle about how some nights, especially during a hard lightning storm, an old 66 Ford pickup, with the round headlights glowing, will come speeding down Route 8. One guy even told me he saw it wreck but when he got to the scene, nothing was there. Just water and fog. They say Luke is still on his way to his girlfriend's house, still driving fast to get there. Let me think, his girlfriend lived out past Union City. Her dad was a Miller. I can't even think of his name, let alone hers."

"It was Mary."

Bill Winston stopped. He stared square at his granddaughter, past her Goth look, her tattoos and the studied air of indifference that she sometimes projected. He saw her as the little girl that she would always be in his eyes - the girl who he taught to play baseball, bait a fish hook and who was growing up way too fast in this troubling world.

"You're right. That was her name."

She lowered her head. "That's what he told me. Luke, the guy who picked me up last night."

Bill opened his arms and Sherry flew into them, softly sobbing. He held her close, rubbing her back and feeling the warmth of his granddaughter's tears as they slid down his cheek, like rain in a storm.

Author Bios

Rex Munsee is an avid reader and hunter, living amid the rolling and forested hills of Western Pennsylvania. Having been born and raised in the foothills of the Appalachian Mountains, he brings a fresh focus to stories he has heard discussed by natives whose roots run deep, and by cops who have patrolled these verdant lands, seeing events in these rural acres that city dwellers wouldn't believe occur...but they do.

Steve Swenston was born in lovely Northern California in the fifties. A lover of the outdoors, television (especially The Outer Limits), art and storytelling, Steve attended junior college and majored in art. Along the way Steve owned a small comic book store, has been published by Marvel Comics, helped start Chaosium Inc., a gaming company, introduced his original creation, Pinsom, to fans of T.S.R. Games, drawn strips for Adventure Gaming Magazine, created educational materials, and taught school art classes.

Jeffrey Vavra has been stringing together letters to make words and saving them up until he had piles of them that he could use to create stories, all the while waiting for just the right moment to unleash them on an Unsuspecting Populace. You, Dear Reader, are that Unsuspecting Populace. You have been warned.

Jeffrey is also the author of the e-book short, THE GAME'S THE THING, where three couples take the party game HOW TO HOST A MURDER MYSTERY to an extreme, and frighteningly logical level, by planning and carrying out murders—For Real! The more elaborate and dangerous the murder, the larger the point value assigned. Who will be the winners? Who will be the losers? Is anyone safe?

Contact Us

We would love to hear from you and what you thought of our stories.

Email: jvavra61@yahoo.com

Website: jeffreyvavra.com

Thanks again for reading.

Rex and Jeffrey

Additional Artwork From Steve

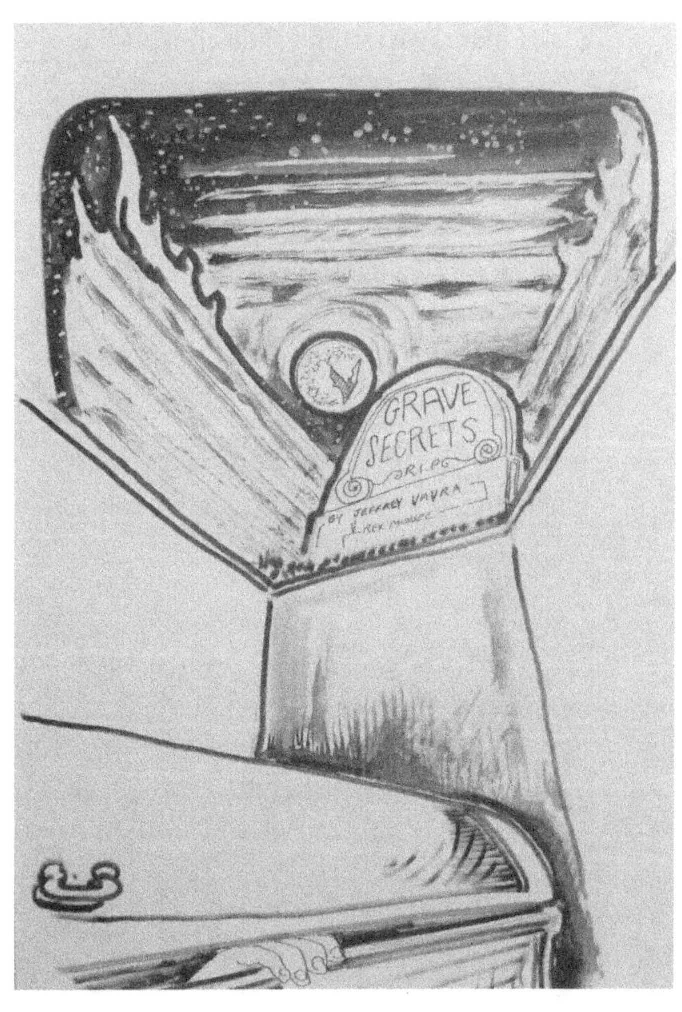

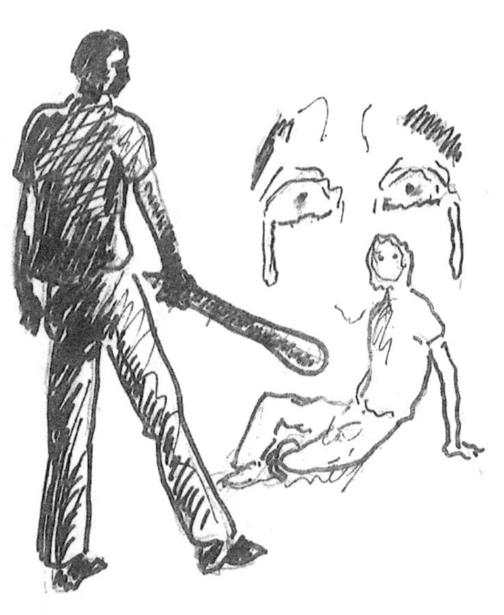

www.ingramcontent.com/pod-product-compliance
Lightning Source LLC
Chambersburg PA
CBHW070909160726
48004CB00003B/1294